Prerequisites for Sleep

Prerequisites for Sleep

Jennifer L. Stone

EDITIONS

Cover design by Doowah Design and Jennifer Stone.

This book was printed on Ancient Forest Friendly paper. Printed and bound in Canada by Hignell Book Printing.

We acknowledge the support of the Canada Council for the Arts and the Manitoba Arts Council for our publishing program.

Library and Archives Canada Cataloguing in Publication

Stone, Jennifer L., 1957-, author
        Prerequisites for sleep / Jennifer L. Stone.

Short stories.
Issued in print and electronic formats.
ISBN 978-1-927426-48-7 (pbk.).
--ISBN 978-1-927426-49-4 (epub)

        I. Title.

PS8637.T6578P74 2014   C813'.6   C2014-905377-0
                                                                        C2014-905378-9

Signature Editions
P.O. Box 206, RPO Corydon, Winnipeg, Manitoba, R3M 3S7
www.signature-editions.com

To the many talented Canadian authors.
I read you and reread you.
You are my teachers.

Contents

Beverly Innes

Beverly Innes was hit by our school bus when she chased an orange kitten onto the road just as the vehicle approached the diner that doubled as her stop. I was sitting in the front seat, behind and to the right of Mr. Amos, the driver, when the words, "Oh, Jesus, no!" left his lips; and he slammed on the brakes, hurling everyone forward, then back, and sending lunch boxes tumbling up the aisle as if they were in a gymnastics competition. After her body flew into the air and landed beneath the path of the right wheel, the bus came to a stop. Through the lower windows of the door, I could see her arm and her leg, bent in an unnatural zigzag shape, and a portion of her blue dress. When I looked up, I saw the kitten run into the ditch on the other side of the road.

I always picture Beverly in that dress, blue with white ruffles down the front. It was the same one she wore in our school photo, taken over forty years ago, when all girls wore dresses to school, most with knee socks that required constant pulling up. A few, pushing their maturity although only eleven, wore nylons, like their mothers. That dress, her dark hair in a pixie cut, a round mouth and large splotchy freckles all over her face. I don't remember the colour of her eyes. They look black in the photo. At the time, I would have described them as beady and her nostrils as flaring; but I could have imagined that, the way children imagine such traits in people they don't like.

It began with a history lesson. We had learned about the cavemen and the natives that inhabited North America. I developed romanticized sympathies for both, knowing that the years would move forward and they would no longer be who they once were. I did not relish the arrival of the French and English and had little patience for discussions about the never-ending disputes between them. On this particular day, the subject was the Jesuit priests who brought Christianity to the New World, and how a number of them were tortured and killed at the hands of the natives.

"Such a tragedy," Mr. Higney, our teacher said, his statement full of saliva as it moved over his tongue. "Such a futile tragedy."

"It was their own fault," I blurted out, letting my sympathies and independent streak get the better of me. "Why didn't they just mind their own business and leave the natives alone?"

The phrase "mind your own business" was one I heard often, every time I let slip, usually at the kitchen table, some piece of information that I thought might liven up our normally quiet meals. Two days previous, I delivered the news, while eating corned beef and cabbage, that according to Ginny Radcliff, the reason Caroline Arsenault went away was that she was going to have twins, then added that I thought she looked fatter the last time I saw her. My grandmother stopped spooning bread and butter pickles onto her plate and held the bottle hovering in mid-air above the table for several seconds before putting it down.

"In this house we mind our own business," my mother said, not acknowledging my comments with eye contact, "meaning we don't voice opinions on the business of others." The kitchen was steamy and warm and full of the smells of spicy boiled meat and vegetables. Her face was flushed, which made her appear more beautiful than she already was. My mother, a commercial artist, was a work of art — every detail, like fine brush strokes, considered for its effect on the overall picture. The best-looking mother in our neighbourhood, she was also the only one that held a job and had her own car.

"If you have something of historical merit to say, Krystal Greenwood, I suggest you try raising your hand." Mr. Higney, a stickler for decorum, glared at me, knowing full well that I had said my piece and would stubbornly refuse to raise my hand, and that he would not favour my outburst with a response.

History class was followed by lunch. I ate my lettuce and Cheez Whiz sandwich, fuming at Mr. Higney and the French. Outside, I stormed around the schoolyard, a noon shadow cringing at my feet, and allowed myself to get good and agitated before coming to a stop next to a group of girls skipping rope by the monkey bars. Two girls held the ends of a fluorescent pink rope while five or six others stood in line waiting to jump. Several glanced in my direction, then returned their attention to the game. They didn't bound or vault into the turning rope, but instead pirouetted on their toes and leapt like ballet dancers. Watching them, I scuffed the gravel with my new sling-back shoes and launched into an anti-meddling rant against the Jesuits.

"Why don't you just shut up?" Beverly said, turning to face me after completing a jump that was almost four feet high. "The Jesuits were spreading the word of Our Heavenly Father. It was important work, so shut up." Her freckles looked like splashes of muddy water on her skin. I could see that the threads holding the ruffle to her dress had come undone, and that there were several holes where the lace had frayed.

I lay crossways on the bed while my mother sat at the dressing table in her room. The bleached room, my grandmother called it. My mother had painted it cool white and adorned it with a white lace bedspread, shams and curtains. Even at seven at night, the westward sun made it as brilliant as a winter day. "So you're going out." I said it with a slight whine in an effort to make her feel guilty. I never really missed her when she went out. It was more of a game I played, trying to get a rise out of her.

"Yes, I'm going out." She clipped emerald green earrings the size of nickels onto her ears and tucked a string of beads under the collar of her blouse. Both were the same colour as her shoes and the skirt that hugged her legs from hips to knees and had a pleated slit up the back that opened when she walked.

I was watching her reflection in the mirror while she put on lipstick. The mirror could be adjusted to imitate different lighting conditions, conditions created by plastic filters sliding in front of fluorescent tubes. The evening setting was a peachy-yellow hue that I associated with birthday candles, the way their flames gave faces a shrouded glow. "When are you coming home?"

"Be good for your grandmother," she said after leaving a candy-apple imprint of her lips on a tissue.

"Will you be back to say goodnight?"

She flipped the mirror over to the magnifying side, picked up her tweezers and leaned forward to pluck a couple of stray eyebrow hairs. "It's a school night. I don't usually get home for goodnights on school nights. You know that." She wiped the dark hairs onto a tissue, then folded it in quarters before dropping it into the wastebasket next to her stool. "So what are you going to watch on television tonight?"

"Red Skelton."

"Why Red Skelton?"

"Because he jumps up in the air and his feet make a clanging noise, like cowbells."

"Cowbells," she said, looking incredulous. "When did you ever hear cowbells?"

At breakfast, she seemed preoccupied, a state that often enabled me to ask her something and get a response that wasn't prefaced by a lecture. I assumed what I believed was my most casual tone, focused on the floral print of the vinyl tablecloth, and said, "How come *we* don't have a Heavenly Father?"

"Because we don't," she said, getting up from the table.

"Why not?"

"Because that's how I like it." She opened the top drawer next to the phone and rooted until she found the Aspirin bottle, then popped tablets alternately with gulps of coffee while mumbling something half under her breath. "Stop dilly-dallying or you'll miss the bus," she said. Then, as if predicting my response, she added, "and I don't have time to drive you to school."

At that point my grandmother shuffled into the kitchen in her nightdress and housecoat. Just past fifty, she was a slightly less curvy, and slightly more wrinkled, version of my mother. "Krystal," she said with a nod, which was the closest thing to good morning I would ever get.

"Don't even think about it," my mother said, catching me before I had a chance to ask my grandmother her opinions on the Heavenly Father.

On Sunday I strolled down the highway and stopped at the lane that led up the hill to the Catholic church. Although it wasn't as large as the Protestant church, its location, overlooking the community, made it appear closer to heaven.

From the bottom of the hill, I gazed up at the white cross that reached towards the heavens and wondered if it ever made contact. I half expected to see it start to glow or be struck by a bolt of lightning. When the doors opened, I slipped between the rows of green community mailboxes, careful not to touch the rusty padlocks, and watched everyone exit in their hats and gloves. They appeared to be stepping off a vessel of some sort, as if they had been away and were now returning from the trip. Some headed straight for their cars and drove off, but others, those who lived close, walked. At first they looked solemn, descending the slope with measured paces until reaching its base, where a transformation of sorts took place. Mothers smiled and children began to giggle and chatter.

The Innes family passed by, close enough that they could have seen me if they looked into the gaps between the mailboxes or peered beneath them where my feet were no doubt visible. "I think," said Mr. Innes, pausing to search his pocket for a smoke, then fumbling with a book of matches before lighting his cigarette, shaking out the flame and tossing the used match into the ditch, "that today we will visit your cousins in the city."

There were seven kids in the Innes family, three girls and four boys. Beverly and her older siblings let out boisterous hoorays while a younger brother wrapped both arms around his father's leg in a hug. The man bent down and ruffled the boy's hair, then picked him up in order to keep walking. After they passed by, I could still hear their laughter as they discussed the games they would play that afternoon and debated who would get the privilege of stretching out on the blanket in the back of their station wagon during the drive.

At school the next day, large raindrops, pelted against the windows by an angry Atlantic wind, kept us in the classroom during breaks. Thirty-three kids with nothing better to do than run up and down and around the rows of wooden desks. Cynthia Grant had twice needed to use the washroom that morning and had unwisely admitted to having the diarrhea. Several girls kept tagging her and passing around diarrhea germs.

"Diarrhea germs! You've got diarrhea germs!" Kathy Williamson tapped my back, then made a gesture of wiping her hands all over my sleeve. "Give them away or they will stay."

I looked around for someone to pass them to and saw Beverly standing at the back of the room. I made a fist when I hit her and saw her wince as she plowed into the bulletin board, forcing art projects askew on their tacks. "Diarrhea germs," I said, "suits your shitty personality."

"Well, at least I'm not stupid." She was blinking away tears while rubbing her arm between her shoulder and elbow.

Beverly was the type of student who worked hard and wouldn't be satisfied with anything less than an

A+. I was mediocre at best, spending most of my time daydreaming or thinking of ways to get out of work. But when it came to comebacks, I was quick. "No, you just look stupid. And you always wear that stupid dress. It's ripped, you know. What's wrong, can't afford thread? Don't you own anything else?"

Her expression flickered between rage and humiliation while she struggled to come up with a retort. Finally she screwed up her face and stuck her tongue out.

"Is that the best you can do?" I said, reiterating the phrase my mother used whenever I got spiteful around her. "Watch this." Then I lifted my head and let my tongue slowly curl out from between my lips before sticking it straight up towards the ceiling. "I'm sticking my tongue out at your Father." Words that sounded like they were spoken by someone with a mouth full of dirty socks.

Proud of my actions, I continued to point my tongue upwards to prolong the effect. All I could hear was our breathing, hers heavy with anger, mine wild with exhilaration. It was almost as if a knob had been turned to lower the volume of everything in the background, or the two of us were inside a glass room, the walls keeping both the noise and other students at bay. When Beverly began to speak, it took half a breath for me to realize that she was talking. "What would you know about fathers?" she whispered. "You wouldn't know your father if you tripped over him. Neither would your mother."

Perhaps it was my stomach that lurched, or my heart that jumped, or my breath that stopped. At the time, I thought it was the ceiling shifting upwards then slamming back down, leaving me with the sensation of being crushed. Here was the manifestation of ideas that had been skirting around in my head for some time. Playing hide-and-seek in the pathways of my cerebrum. Thoughts that I believed only I considered. Things no one else would bother to waste time on. Why would they?

I pretended I didn't hear Beverly, slowly lowering my head until my tongue was level with her eyes then spinning on my heels and running off to distribute more diarrhea germs to some other unsuspecting classmate.

We were led off the bus through the emergency exit at the back and taken into the diner. Beverly's body was covered with a blanket and half obscured behind a police cruiser by the time another bus arrived to take us to school. Her sobbing mother and siblings were comforted by neighbours. In those days, life went on as usual. There were never school closures or trauma counsellors rushed to the scene. Our history and math and English lessons were still carried out, although perhaps in a more sombre tone; and by the following morning, Mr. Amos was back behind the wheel of our school bus, which was newly washed to remove any evidence.

Had I wished her dead? Sure I had, the same way any child would make such a wish through gritted teeth. Did I feel guilty? Not in the least. It was not guilt I felt the next day when the entire school stood for two minutes, and I concentrated on the brown and tan tiles of the floor, moving my eyes along the squares like chess pieces while my classmates moved their lips silently through prayers. I knew that wishes didn't come true. If they did, my mother would have come into my room one night and sat on the edge of my bed, the way I always wanted her to, and explained why I had no father or grandfather or extended family to speak of. Why we lived almost mute in a house where my grandmother, my mother, and I all shared the same last name. Instead, I was conscious of something else, something I would experience again and again over the course of my lifetime, not a feeling of loss, but a sense of never having had, not belonging to any entity greater than myself. It was the loneliest feeling in the world.

Billy

I'm sitting in the front passenger seat of our van, a seventeen-year-old Dodge Caravan, the most popular minivan ever sold, according to Billy. This one is rusty and probably won't pass its next safety inspection. Lucy is on my lap, the two of us squished into one seat belt. I know this is illegal, but Amy, Charlotte, and Eli are in the back along with Grapefruit, our mixed-breed dog, who likes to slobber all over the place. Already the van is beginning to smell like dog saliva and sweat. Further back is all our stuff, a few suitcases and an entire package of green garbage bags with our clothes and lots of sheets and towels and other household items that Ma stuffed into them when she ran around the house screaming at Billy and calling him an effing no-good piece of shit.

Ma is turning the key and the ignition is clicking and clicking. Sometimes it will take several minutes of turning and clicking before it catches. She is cursing under her breath, like she doesn't want anyone to hear her, which makes me wonder if she remembers that only forty minutes ago she was expressing every four-letter word known to man at top volume. I had to cover Lucy's ears with my hands 'cause she is only four and didn't need to hear all that. Eli is nine, and he didn't need to hear all that either; but I couldn't cover two sets of ears at the same time, so I just motioned with my head for him to follow me outside, while I headed for the door stooped over Lucy so I could keep my hands on her ears as she walked. We went over to the swing set, where I held Lucy on my lap with my arms wrapped around the chains and my hands still over her ears. She was thinking it was some kind of game and giggled and squirmed a bit, but not enough to make my hands slip from where I held them. Eli sat and twisted the swing in semicircles back and forth while he scuffed his running shoes in the worn spot where there is no grass under the swings. We could still hear Ma swearing, only at a lower volume.

Billy is standing outside the van in bare feet. I can see tears flowing down his cheeks. He is twitching, like he needs a cigarette or a drink. He has been trying to quit both. He told me yesterday that he has been off the bottle for two months, six days, and fourteen hours, but is having a little trouble with the cigarettes.

Billy is the closest thing I have to a dad. My real father, Rod, is gone, to Calgary, I think. I haven't seen him since I was about three years old. I couldn't even tell you what he looks like except that he must look somewhat like me because sometimes Ma gets mad and tells me to stop looking at her like that, and I say like what? and she says like your father. I don't have any pictures to see exactly which parts of us look the same.

Charlotte is three years older than me, and Amy is four years younger. They both have Clyde for a father. Ma married Clyde when she was pregnant with Charlotte. Then she left Clyde and moved in with Rod, stayed a few years and had me. When she left Rod, she was still married to Clyde so we all went to live with him. Amy was born the following year. I never felt close enough to Clyde to think he could be a replacement father. On a scale of one to ten, Clyde was a four point five. He never really bothered with us kids, except when he yelled for us to get our grubby paws off his car. Clyde was more interested in sex and beer and sometimes pickup hockey, when it didn't interfere with sex and beer. Billy once said that Clyde was a cliché. I think I know what he was getting at. I could never figure out myself why it took Ma over five years to get tired of it all the second time round, when surely she would have known what she was getting into.

Billy is Eli's real dad, so Eli is kind of upset back there because he has never experienced the up and leaving that Ma has a habit of doing. I know he's trying real hard not to cry, or at least not cry too loud. His forehead is pressed against the window and his eyes are shut so tight they look like they hurt. Every so often I hear a partially suppressed sniffle.

Eli and Billy are pretty close. They go fishing and play lots of video games together. Sometimes Eli and Billy go away, just the two of them, on what Billy calls a boys' weekend. I don't know what they do for the entire two days, but I do know Eli gets pretty excited every time they start planning one. I figure it must be like an extended sleepover, where they stay up really late and eat a lot of junk food and do crazy things that they don't have to explain to anyone. I did see Billy pack his rifle last time and have to admit that I wished I could have gone with them, just once, 'cause taking potshots at cans seems like a whole lot more fun than painting toenails and applying fake tattoos.

Billy has been pretty good to us, considering. Except for Eli, who is still fairly young, we weren't the best-behaved kids. I skipped a lot of school to drink, toke, and do plenty of other stuff with Brian Simpson, things that scare the crap out of me when I think about Lucy ever doing them. All that stopped when I got pregnant. Now I'm trying really hard to be a good parent, which I have to do by myself 'cause Brian wouldn't believe me when I told him that he was the only person I ever had sex with. He called me some not very nice names, and that's when I decided that I didn't want him to be the other parent anyway. Ma didn't say much, other than I better get used to changing shitty diapers; but Billy told me that I was strong enough to do it on my own and that Lucy still had a family.

You wouldn't know it by looking at him, 'cause he appears pretty down and out, but Billy has a university degree. It shows sometimes when he's talking serious and his sentences get peppered with big words. The last real serious talk he had with me was about six months ago when he suggested I take something called the GED. He and Ma had just had a big fight about Amy 'cause she was skipping classes and doing things with Brian Simpson's younger brother Gil that she shouldn't be doing. Ma told him to mind his own GD business 'cause Amy was her kid, not his, and he had no right to interfere. When Billy mentioned the GED, I looked at him like I always do when he talks about things that I don't understand, so he explained it some more. He said that it was a high school diploma test. If I passed it, it would mean that I graduated from high school and I would be able to get a better job or, if I wanted to, go on to college or university. It would mean I would be able to take better care of Lucy in the future. I don't want to sound pessimistic, he said, but things happen. If you have some education, it will be a lot easier to get yourself and Lucy out of a situation you don't want to be in. Billy offered to help me and bought the book when he drove to Halifax one day to pick up some parts for his truck. We have been working on the practice problems ever since. I have an appointment to take the test a week from Wednesday. Billy said he would drive me there and take Lucy to a movie while I did the writing.

Lucy adores Billy. He pushes her on the swings and takes her fishing with him and Eli. Last winter, when she had a really bad cold and looked like Rudolph the Red-Nosed Reindeer, he bought her a box of Puffs tissues 'cause they have lotion in them and would be softer on her nose. You would have thought he gave her a gold brick the way she held onto that box, sleeping with it and gently packing it into her Dora the Explorer knapsack whenever she had to go anywhere. Up until this morning, it was still somewhere in our room with the last tissue in the bottom 'cause she didn't want it to be empty and have to throw it in the garbage.

Right now Lucy is silent and not moving, which is how I know she is upset 'cause normally she fidgets and asks a billion questions. She is sideways, facing the passenger window with her head tucked into the space between my boob and armpit. I keep playing with the curls in her hair, trying to distract her a little bit and let her know that I'm here for her.

After I had Lucy, Billy never once said anything about having another kid in the house and another mouth to feed. He did say in the middle of an argument with Ma that he didn't want another one of us kids doing something stupid with some horny teenager who would never live up to their responsibility. I didn't ask him, but I'm pretty sure the *another one* he was referring to is Amy, and I can understand that, even though I love Lucy to death and would never consider giving her up, 'cause I know my life is going to be a whole lot different than how I thought it would be back when I was in school.

Amy can't understand this right now 'cause she is in the middle of her toking, drinking, and fooling-around-without-thinking stage. When I try to talk to her, 'cause I've been there, she tells me to shut my effing trap and mind my own GD business. Amy sure can swear. She's a lot like Ma in that way. She is also really pretty, like the pictures of Ma when she was younger. I'm not saying that any of us are ugly, but Amy is definitely the prettiest. I overheard Mrs. MacLeod, who lives across the road, say that Amy was far too pretty for her own good. That spells T-R-O-U-B-L-E, she said right before she saw me standing by the milk cooler at the variety store. Then she shut up and pretended she didn't see me; but I know she did because before she stopped talking she had added the words, *just like*, to her sentence.

Charlotte is really pissed at Billy right now so I know she doesn't care whether Ma leaves or not. Charlotte moved back in with us after her husband Chester was convicted of burning down a mobile home belonging to Harold Richards. Harold's daughter Wendy and her boyfriend Norman King were living there at the time. The rumours said that Chester burnt them out because they owed him some money. The rumours also said that it was money for coke. The worst thing about the whole situation was that Wendy and Norman were passed out in the trailer when it burnt and now they are both in pretty rough shape. This got Chester sent away for attempted murder, and Harold mad as hell at Billy, who used to maintain all his trucks and construction equipment. Now Billy works at the fish plant, a low-wage, seasonal job that doesn't allow him to use his best skill: the ability to keep motors going in cars, trucks, lawn tractors, chainsaws or any other electrical or gas-powered machine you can name, long after most people would junk them and buy new ones.

The reason Charlotte is so angry is that Chester is getting out of prison in a couple weeks, and she figured that he was going to come live here with all of us until the two of them worked out what they were going to do. Ma didn't seem to have a problem with this, but when Billy found out, which wasn't until this morning, he put his foot down and said that there was no way in hell that Chester was staying under his roof, and if Ma wanted to welcome somebody like that into the house after all the things he did, then she better find another house to live in.

That's when Ma started her cursing and screaming at Billy and gathering things into garbage bags, 'cause Ma is like a wild animal when it comes to her kids. When she gets her hackles up, there is no way that anyone will stop her from doing what it takes to make sure they get what they want. That's just the way she is. It's the way she's always been. Right around then, when I was stooped over Lucy, protecting her ears from all the swearing, I realized I had never mentioned to Ma how much I wanted to take that test.

I'm staring out the window at Billy. He is standing on the grass. His nose is running and he wipes it on the sleeve of his denim shirt. I want to smile and raise my hand in a half wave but Ma is watching. The engine catches, then stalls, and Ma swears again, this time not under her breath. She turns the key once more and the van coughs and sputters back to life. Eli begins to sob real loud in the back seat. Grapefruit, being sympathetic, 'cause Eli is his favourite person in the whole world, starts to whine. Then Ma pumps the gas pedal and the engine revs, almost loud enough to drown it all out.

Shades of Pink

Several months ago, Andy and I moved in together. Before that we had existed in two apartments for over a year. Some of my clothes were in his closet, and a great deal of his stuff was stored at my place. One day, we drove up the 404, Andy behind the wheel of his newly leased Ford, took the exit at Newmarket and continued northward until we found a house we could afford. This particular house, constructed in the early '70s, was well kept, with new doors and windows and ceramic and hardwood floors as recent upgrades. Andy wanted a kitchen large enough to add his dream island. This one fit the bill.

Andy works as an apprentice chef at an upscale restaurant in a downtown hotel. He rarely has a night off. We had re-met on one of those rare nights, when I bumped into him at a party that I attended with my friend Steph. He was leaning against the wall by the bathroom door, waiting to get in. Happy to be on my way out, I practically knocked him over. "Hey, I know you. Lisa, right?" In a previous life called college, Andy studied culinary arts and I took costume design, a single English class being the only thing we had in common. He had an easy appearance and a demeanour that was goofy but nice. During my college days, I had been too busy to notice such things.

I peddle my services to theatre companies and festivals and am often hired in the costume departments of movies that take place in Toronto. Stephanie and I are currently working on the same production, glorified dressers of elves in a made-for-TV Christmas movie. Sipping coffee outside a trailer on Queen West, we watch curious pedestrians, who slow their pace around us, hoping to spot someone famous, or at least someone wearing fake snow and a winter jacket in July.

"How's life with Andy?" she says.

"Great. He spoils me rotten. He doesn't work until later in the day but still gets up most mornings and does breakfast. Today he made poached eggs on toast with an amazing herb sauce and peach cobbler. And you should see my lunch. Living with a guy who cooks certainly has its perks."

Coffee slurps over the Styrofoam rim of her cup. "What about the drive?"

"It's a drag. There's always traffic to contend with and bad weather. I'd take the Go Train, but you know how it is, the hours aren't exactly standard. During my last contract, I had to be on location by 6:00 a.m. Plus,

I need my car to pick up fabric and notions at various locations in the city."

"So why are you living way up there? Think about it, Lisa. It's tough enough to have a career in this business."

"We like it there. We have so much space, and a backyard with a maple tree. Andy wants to plant some vegetables next year."

"Are you guys for real?" Steph tries to make it sound like she's kidding. I have been around her long enough to know better.

A week later, the movie has wrapped and I am looking at a small ad in the Newmarket paper, nothing spectacular, one column wide, a few lines deep. *Wanted, designer for three-dimensional advertising products. Must have pattern drafting and sewing experience. Call Magnus Johannsson.* I dial the number. Within an hour, I'm holding the directions in front of me, pressing the slip of paper into the steering wheel with my thumb at the two-o'clock position and glancing down to check the trip meter. Take Mount Albert Road east at Leslie, drive about five kilometres, look for brick farmhouse on the north side. The meter reads 4.8 when I first see the house.

The property is large, with a long driveway. Subdivisions are encroaching from both the south and the east. The west and north directions are still open. Who knows for how long? I park and fetch my portfolio from the back seat. There is a sunroom across the front of the house. It's obviously an add-on, but nicely done. When I knock, a clanging sound of pots comes from somewhere inside, then two sets of feet across a wooden floor, a scamper and a stride. A woman and a girl of about three appear at the door.

"Hi, I'm Zoe," the child says, wrapping her finger in a blonde curl.

Smiling, I direct my words towards the woman eyeing me through the screen. She is holding the door handle but makes no effort to turn it. I feel as if an important button on my blouse is undone or there is something unpleasant hanging from my nose. "I have an appointment with Magnus Johannsson."

"That's my daddy!" Zoe is bouncing on her toes with a head full of yellow slinkies.

"In the workshop," the woman says and jerks her head towards the back of the house.

The driveway leads to a large white building. In a skirt and heels, it is difficult to walk on the gravel. I should have known better. He told me I was coming to a farmhouse.

The door opens before I get there and a man greets me with his hand extended and a smile that stretches across his face. "You must be Lisa." The accent I detected on the phone sounds more pronounced. Before I can answer, he takes my hand and shakes it vigorously, to the point that I fear for my arm. "You brought something for me to see."

"Yes, my portfolio."

"Very good, let's take a look."

Inside the building, fluorescent lights buzz above my head and rolls of material lean against plywood walls. Some of the rolls are shiny, like waterproofed windbreakers. Others have a flat finish.

"What kind of fabric do you use?"

"Nylon," says Magnus. "We have two types."

"What's the difference?"

He points to a roll with the dull finish. "This is for my balloon."

Before I can digest the word *balloon*, he leads me into an office and clears space on a cluttered desk, then sits next to me at the front. We are so close that I slide my legs away and my left knee rubs against the wood. Slowly he turns the pages that hold my sketches and photos. When he is finished, he closes the portfolio and I wait for his words.

"When can you start?" he says, drumming his fingers on the back cover.

"Right away."

"Good, start tomorrow." Both his voice and expression are deadpan.

"But what exactly will I be doing?" I'm so stunned that my words come out like popping bubbles.

At this, Magnus laughs. His eyes twinkle and I laugh too. Then we talk, both of us talking much too fast, for a couple of hours.

Before I leave, he shows me around and introduces me to the seamstresses. May is cheerful with flushed, menopausal cheeks. She chats for a few minutes before returning to her work. Lin, the name an abbreviated version of something longer, is originally from Thailand. She offers a shy smile and a nod of her head.

Shortly after midnight, Andy comes home from work. I'm propped up on the bed, trying to read. My adrenalin is pumping too fast to concentrate on the text. "I have a new job." I blurt it out before he kisses me.

"Already? It usually takes you a couple of weeks." He sneaks in the kiss and I take a breath.

"This one is full-time and close, ten minutes, tops!"

Andy peels off his shirt and lets his jeans fall to the floor. As a chef, he is conscious of how easy it is to put on a few extra pounds so he exercises every morning after I leave for work. I pause to appreciate the moment as he crawls in beside me with his boxers on.

"It's a dream job, designing advertising inflatables, three-dimensional shapes that fill with air when they are connected to a fan."

"Won't they explode?" He begins to plant kisses in the vicinity of my left ear.

"No, they have zippers and vents, plus some of the air leaks out the seams. My boss is a famous balloonist from Iceland. You should see him. What a character."

"I think this calls for a celebration." He slips his hands under my T-shirt and skims my face with his lips.

"You smell like chocolate," I tell him and we both laugh.

For the first few days, Magnus instructs me in the physics of inflatables and the need for reinforcements and baffles — inside walls that force them to keep a desired shape. Without them, everything would be round. When he isn't available, I help May and Lin mend older inflatables. On the morning of my fourth day, I am sitting at a sewing machine when Magnus approaches, stops and looms above me. He is cartoonish in appearance, round eyes behind aviator-rimmed glasses and a fixed smile that pushes his cheeks back to his ears, Iceland's version of the Grinch after returning Christmas to Whoville. He is tall and lanky, with thick blond hair that looks like it was cut with a mixing bowl. I have come to the conclusion that style means nothing to him. He has too many other things to do. For someone only nine years older than I am, he has accomplished so much more, including breaking the world altitude record in a hot air balloon. "Lisa, I have decided on your first project," he says.

"This is good news." I try to sound confident, but my stomach is immediately invaded by Mexican jumping beans that can't decide whether they are excited or anxious.

"I would like a large cake, three tiers with icing and candles, something that can be rented out for celebrations. Each tier should also be able to hold a six-foot-high banner. Is that possible?"

A cake. I'm pretty sure I can make a cake, at least one out of fabric. The beans in my stomach slow to a skip. "I don't see why not. I can break it down into basic shapes. Let me do some sketches to show you."

It is easy to tell that Magnus is pleased. When I show him my sketches, he looks like an excited little boy with dollar signs in his eyes. "How much time will it take?"

"I don't really know. I've never done anything like this before."

"Take Lin when you're ready. She's fast and can help sew it."

I do the math first, the circumferences and diameters that make up the shapes, additional measurements for inside baffles. These are easy; large rectangles of fabric sewn together can make cylinders for the layers; giant donuts and circles will do for the tops. The same idea will work for the candles. Based on the circumferences, I draft patterns for wavy tubes that will create two colours of piped icing. Then I design faux-icing flowers to be made from twelve petal-shaped pieces.

In a few days, Lin and I are cutting and sewing yellow nylon to create sixty-eight flowers. Lin is a lot faster than I am. She brushes aside my words when I thank her. I try to engage her in conversation, succeeding when I ask about kids. She has two, one in university and one finishing high school. "I'm a proud mother," she says. "My children are my greatest accomplishment, but they are a lot of work. No matter how hard you try, you can never tell how they will turn out."

"Like inflatables," I say, but she doesn't smile and I realize I am making light of something she takes very seriously. "Only harder," I tack on.

It takes the two of us three weeks working flat out to build the cake. I can't sleep at night for fear it will fall apart or fail to inflate properly. I get a cold and my nose runs constantly and turns bright pink. Andy makes me hot rum toddies and rubs all the right places to help me relax. He comes to work with me on the morning the cake is going to be inflated.

"This is Andy, my better half," I say to Magnus. He is puzzled by my colloquial expression. "My boyfriend," I say. Then Andy looks puzzled. This is not a term we've ever used. "We live together. He came to see my cake." Magnus nods and walks to the fan and plugs it in.

When the air starts to enter the pile of fabric, I hold my breath. We watch as the layers slowly rise upwards. Then each icing tube and yellow blossom takes shape, reminding me of a slow-motion nature sequence on TV. For a moment, we are suspended in time as we wait for the candles to stand up on top. They bounce into position and I imagine a cartoon *boing*. I jump up and down and hug Andy while Magnus tethers it to a couple of trees, then crawls inside to check the baffles. When he comes out, he says nothing, but I recognize his look.

"It's amazing," says Andy. "When it started to rise, it actually looked like it was baking, like it contained yeast or baking powder. And I thought you couldn't cook."

Later, Andy is making us a special dinner to mark the occasion. I watch him cutting celery, mesmerized by how he rolls the knife on the curve of the blade with one hand and slowly advances the stalks with the other. There is no chopping sound, just a slice of stainless steel and a green crunch. This is his art. I am sitting on a tall stool next to the island, jabbering on about my cake, when it registers that I am bordering on annoying so I change the subject.

"You never tell me about your work."

He stops and looks up. "Not much to tell. I go into the kitchen. I cook someone else's menu, then I leave." He finishes the celery and reaches for a package of chicken livers. "A chef doesn't really exist unless he is cooking his own creations."

The next day Magnus tells me that the cake has been rented for the weekend and we need to create the banners. He hands me a paper with the words HONEST AL'S BIRTHDAY SALE, and tells me to have Lin do them. He is smiling more widely than usual, something I didn't think was possible. "I should take you up in the balloon," he says.

"Really! What's it like?"

"Peaceful. You're drifting above the earth with only a basket between you and falling. Of course, things appear small, but not like when you see them from a plane — there is no glare from glass, so things have more depth. People sometimes reach out to try to touch them. For some reason, they need to make sure they are real. Some people can get carried away and you have to pull them back."

"Sounds surreal."

"I'll take you sometime so you can experience it for yourself."

When I turn around, Magnus's wife, Joanne, is glaring at me. She is sitting at the front desk training Nancy, the new secretary. Nancy is focused on the phone in front of her as if it is about to grow legs and walk away.

On Monday, I arrive early to review my documentation on the cake. With written instructions and diagrams, May and Lin will create additional inventory. As I walk by his office, Magnus calls out to me. He is sitting at his desk, which is unusual, because Magnus is too hyper to sit still. Outside, it is raining and water is dripping from my jacket. I wipe away a drop that lands on my cheek and push my hood back.

"Do you think you can design an elephant?" he asks.

I take a moment to think. "Sitting down would be best."

"Yes, sitting down is best. Can it be done?"

"Sure, why not?"

At the drafting table, doodling some rough elephants, I hope I'm not getting too cocky. This could prove to be much harder than a cake. Magnus comes by and looks at my sketches. "This elephant that you're making, what colour nylon should I order?"

"Pink."

"Why pink?" he says, wrinkling his nose so that he looks like an animated rabbit.

"Haven't you ever heard of pink elephants?"

"No."

"They're an illusion. When someone has too much to drink, they begin to see things that aren't there, like blue mice and pink elephants. If you really want some publicity, you could put one up at the top of the Don Valley where the highways all merge, and have banners that read DON'T DRINK AND DRIVE."

He looks at me like I am speaking a foreign language.

After work, I go to Toys "R" Us at the mall. The stuffed animal section is next to the baby products, just past bikes and outdoor toys. A little boy is riding a big-wheel trike up the aisle. His bum is only inches off the floor while his feet man the pedals on the large front tire. The noise rumbles through the store.

I pick up a small elephant that is white with contrasting blue striped fabric on the undersides of its ears and the pads of its feet. Its trunk is up and I decide to buy it. I've read somewhere that elephants with their trunks up are lucky.

When Andy comes home from work he points to the elephant sitting on our dresser. "What's this?" He tosses his cooking whites into the laundry basket. I catch a whiff of someone else's menu. Garlic and onions and curry, and the lingering smell of cooking oil — too much oil. Andy would never overuse cooking oil in his own creations. "Is there something you want to tell me?" His eyes light up, and he delivers a grin that says he could handle it if I were to spring certain news.

"It's my inspiration. I'm making a twenty-five-foot pink elephant."

"Hey," he laughs, "you could put it next to the highway during the holidays with a DON'T DRINK AND DRIVE banner."

"That's exactly what I said, but Magnus didn't get it. He didn't understand the connotation, even after I explained it."

"Did you tell him it would make the news?"

"I tried, but he has an entirely different thought process; and I don't think pro bono is his style."

On Thursday, Joanne seeks me out to give me my pay. She works an hour a day in the shop, taking care of the money and the books. She is the opposite of Magnus, serious and tense with unruly brown hair. Shadowed crescents below her eyes give her a hollow look, although overall, she is an attractive woman. With makeup and hot rollers, she would be beautiful. I heard her tell Nancy the story of how Magnus swept her off her feet in a balloon when she was backpacking with friends through Europe.

"Did you like the cake?" I ask when she hands me an envelope.

"I like the idea of the cake," she says. "It will be good for business."

Forcing a smile, I thank her for my pay and decide to save any future questions for Zoe, who brings me pictures and tells me that I should make them into inflatables. They all look the same, triangle bodies with big eyes. She has the basic shape right — inflatables need large bottoms.

The elephant is coming along nicely, although I lie awake at night correcting design flaws. I make a small-scale model, stuffed with cotton fluff, to test a pattern I drafted on graph paper. Magnus runs a low-tech shop, so to create the full-scale version I have to grid up the pattern manually. This requires taping together large pieces of heavy brown paper and using bricks and boards to hold it flat because it constantly wants to curl. The second step is measuring and drawing the lines to create giant graph paper. Afterwards there is the process of filling in the large boxes with the same information that is on my miniature version. It's not difficult, only time-consuming and hard on the knees and neck. I plug away at it while humming the jingle from an old cereal commercial. *Pink elephants, pink, pink elephants, lots of pink elephants…*

Magnus, antsy as he is, checks on my progress about thirty times a day. He crouches on his haunches a couple of feet from where I am trying to work.

"So when do I get that balloon ride?" I keep trying to make conversation because if I don't, he just sits there watching me with his happy-Grinch grin.

"When you finish your elephant."

"Is that a promise?"

"I give you my word."

"Good, an incentive plan. If I don't like it, you'll have to come up with different rewards for future projects. How about cash bonuses?"

"You'll like it."

"Company shares?"

"You are such a dreamer."

"Ah, but you like my dreams because I dream in 3D."

"Stop dreaming and build your elephant." He laughs as he gets up and walks away.

May and Lin are making a cake, so I surround myself with pink nylon and sew the elephant on my own. A cylinder-shaped baffle runs through the centre and reinforcements are necessary on the trunk and neck. For contrast, I make the insides of the ears and the toenails purple. I'm glad to be off my knees and the job goes quickly.

"I wish you didn't have to work today," I say to Andy over an apple-crêpe breakfast. "Once I attach all the loops, we're going to inflate my elephant."

"Take the video camera; we'll watch it as soon as I get home. We can have popcorn to celebrate. I'll pick up the candy-coated stuff you like from Kernels."

Later, May operates the video camera so I can see the elephant inflate at actual size. Magnus connects the fan and turns it on. The body begins to unfold, taking shape like an embryo developing its parts. My stomach clenches when the head and trunk emerge and I worry about pressure on the seams of the neck and gusset. In less than two minutes, the large ears snap into place and my pachyderm is sitting large and pink before me — smiling.

Magnus is pleased. "Looks excellent," he says, walking around and surveying the body from all angles. "Nice big ears for banners. And you gave him a tail."

"Her. I gave her a tail. Can't imagine a pink elephant being a him."

"Perhaps you wish to name *her*."

"Perhaps."

"Come, let's check to see how *she* is holding up."

Undoing the back zipper, we crawl inside and stand up. The fan hums and cool air brushes my skin. Magnus closes the zipper and pulls on the baffle that stretches from the elephant's neck to the canvas base, then inspects the flat-felled seams of the outer walls.

"You don't make mistakes," he says. That little-boy look is on his face.

"I do. I make hundreds. I just make them over and over in my head. I try to think things through before I jump in."

Without warning he wraps me in his arms and kisses me. His breath smells like Juicy Fruit. I try to recall if I have ever seen him chew gum. He kisses me again, this time it is long and passionate. I blink and struggle to focus. Everything around me is pink. I think about Andy at work, not existing among someone else's creations, and about drifting in a balloon. I reach out and try to touch something real. There is no one there to pull me back.

Prerequisites for Sleep

It rained through the night and early morning, tearing the petals from the lilies in the garden. They lay on the ground like pieces of satin tinged with rust. The sky looked bruised, as if it had more crying to do. Anita stood in the kitchen, looking out at the day through the screen of the back door. The thin lines of mesh made everything appear slightly out of focus.

"Some people believe that it is good luck to have rain on your wedding day," Judith said cheerfully.

Anita poured coffee into her favourite mug, a black one with a large white A on the side and a chip in the rim, then sat down at the table next to her aunt. Lately, she thought of her aunt as Saint Judith, Saint Jude for short. What else could she be after taking on the responsibility of raising Anita when her mother and father died? Judith had given up the career of an overseas correspondent to become a weekly columnist and an instant parent. In fourteen years, Anita had never heard her aunt complain. Any regrets, if she had them, were not voiced.

"Kevin's mother has rented enough tents to create an upscale refugee camp," Anita said, scooping two heaping teaspoons of sugar into her coffee.

"It is nice of the Sinclairs to host the wedding," Judith ventured. "Kevin's a dear, but you know we would have never been able to put on a spread for that family. Oh, they are always pleasant to everyone and not snobby by any means, but they are used to certain things. Do me a favour, don't get so used to certain things that you won't eat my macaroni and cheese casserole."

"Well, Kevin is her only child," Anita said. "Some women like taking care of such details. I'm not one of them. The things I decided to take care of are more than enough wedding details for me. And I don't think you have to worry about the casserole. It's still my favourite." The spoon, hitting the mug as she stirred, underlined her words with porcelain-steel music.

"I know what you mean about wedding details," said Judith. "They aren't my forte, that's for sure."

"Do you ever wish that you had married?" Anita said. She searched her aunt's face as she posed the question. Up until she was sixteen, Anita would look for her mother in Judith's face, but the more she had looked the more she noticed the differences between the two sisters. What she saw these days was that the years had been good to Judith. Her mother, no longer accumulating time, existed only in the photo albums and old videos stored in the hall closet.

"Oh, I think if the right person had come along, I would have married," said Judith, "but who's to say that the right person can't still show up? Fifty-two is not that old, you know." Her voice shifted and she leaned back in the kitchen chair to look directly at her niece. "Don't go thinking that you're the reason I didn't get married. I had plenty of offers, just none that I could live with."

Anita brushed her teeth and stepped into the shower, surveying her body as she adjusted the water temperature. She had put on a few pounds since they announced the engagement, but not a noticeable amount. At her final fitting last week, the dress was perfect. How lucky that she had been able to find one she liked that was on sale.

It was at a little boutique that Kevin's mother had recommended, located in Barberry Market, an area of old stone houses that had been turned into upscale businesses. The signs hanging from each were understated and catered to a clientele that didn't need to be shouted at. Anita drove down with Judith one afternoon, thinking they would just look. They found a parking spot on the other side of a street split by a median with a couple of benches and some annual beds. It was the end of April and the empty gardens filled the air with an organic smell of damp soil.

They looked at several dresses, but Anita kept coming back to the same one. "Go ahead, try it on," the woman said, unzipping the clear plastic so the gown could be viewed better.

Her reflection: auburn hair, freckled skin, white dress, shouted at her without words. Was she ready for this? She didn't know whether to laugh or cry.

"It suits you," Judith said.

"This particular gown is part of a special promotion," the salesclerk said. "Reduced because of the arrival of new stock."

Today that special promotion was hanging on the back of her bedroom door.

They met the rest of the girls at the beauty salon at eleven, Anita's friends Ingrid and Wendy, and Kevin's cousin Michelle.

Ingrid greeted them with exaggerated hugs and kisses that made Anita feel like a plush toy that had been returned after an unplanned absence. "You do realize," Ingrid teased, "that by this time tomorrow you will no longer be a single entity but part of a pair."

Wendy laughed. "Like shoes."

"Or salt and pepper shakers," said Michelle.

"I don't know if I should be jealous or relieved," said Ingrid.

By the time they left the salon, the sky was clear, the sidewalks nothing but strips of glare. Anita wondered whether or not this had any bearing on her luck, now that both the sun and the rain had made an appearance on her wedding day.

"Just in time for photos," Judith said. Leave it to Judith to say the right thing.

Judith excelled at saying the right thing. After the funeral, she and Anita had returned to the house, which was empty for the first time in days. Someone had tidied up, depriving them of the much-needed busywork. Anita flopped down on the sofa, no longer feeling like the preteen who, just the previous week, had gone to a sleepover with her friends. She had returned the following morning to find a police car waiting in the driveway. Anita resented the loss of her childhood almost as much as she resented her absent mother and father and the stoned kid who ran the red light. Judith came in and sat down next to her. "I always wanted to learn how to play one of those things," she said, pointing to the Nintendo system on the shelf below the TV. "How 'bout we order a pizza and you can teach me?"

That night they slowly allowed themselves to laugh and yell at the characters that jumped across the television screen, and then to slip into a realm where silliness prevailed. Afterwards they slept, waking late the following day with a new understanding of the roles they had inherited in each other's lives, knowing that anything either one of them did from now on would affect the other.

Judith gave her away. That was something that Anita had insisted on and Kevin agreed. It was only right. They walked down the aisle arm in arm amidst harp music and the rustle of satin and silk, neither one shaking or teary-eyed, no mention of what Anita's mother or father might have felt. There was no need to; they had stopped dwelling on the past years before.

"Kevin's uncle Gerald would be glad to walk you down the aisle," his mother had suggested, along with several other options, all male, as dictated by tradition. His mother was not one for altering institutions. But she was also not one for fighting small battles, so in the end she agreed.

Mrs. Sinclair liked Anita and thought of her as hard-working and smart, not some spoiled bimbo who couldn't see past her next visit to the spa. Although she had always been well-off, the older woman had learned the same lessons that Anita had at an early age; that nothing was to be taken for granted, and that important things can disappear, the way her brother had disappeared into the river; and afterwards, the way her mother had disappeared into the bottle. Of all the girls that Kevin had been involved with, Anita had the most substance. The least she could do for the girl was give her a beautiful wedding. And a beautiful wedding dress, for that matter; no one needed to know of the arrangement made between her and the owner of the boutique.

"I think I'm switching to autopilot," Kevin whispered in her ear partway through the receiving line.

Anita smiled. She could think of nothing better than sitting down and putting her feet up. "Tell me again why we didn't elope," she whispered back, while waiting for his grandfather to close the gap in the stream of people. Kevin laughed and bent to kiss her enthusiastically on the mouth. The room burst into a round of applause.

"Okay, break it up," said Kevin's grandfather, leaning forward to peck Anita on the cheek.

Next in line was Richard. His face, like a statue with stone eyes and a rigid jaw, moved towards her. "Will you be going by Mrs. Sinclair now, or do you intend to keep your own name?" His question surprised her.

At dinner, Judith made a speech that was both happy and sad. She talked about their life together and about new beginnings, the one they undertook fourteen years earlier and the one that Anita and Kevin were now embarking on. "I believe that Anita can manage anything that comes her way, including you, Kevin," she quipped, a statement that was followed by laughter, along with whoops and whistles from Kevin's friends.

The rest of the day went off without a hitch. Everyone would remember it as a lovely event. Mrs. Sinclair had taken their wishes and transformed them into a choreographed work of art. Anita tried to imagine how Kevin's mother would use those skills on the many committees and boards that she was a member of.

She was curled up in the king-size bed next to Kevin. He had slipped quickly into sleep after they had made love. To her, sleep didn't arrive as easily so she slid out from under the covers and pulled on the complimentary terry robe. The hotel room was on the top floor, overlooking the harbour. A fog rolled above the water, looking pinkish-yellow from city lights that never allow darkness to settle or stars to shine. Standing in the window, Anita continued to revisit the day in her thoughts. For her this was a nightly habit, rehashing the events of her life in twenty-four-hour segments, one of her prerequisites for sleep.

Richard had come to the wedding. Richard, who got through university the way she did, on part-time jobs and student loans, barely making ends meet as he worked his way towards being a heart specialist. She knew he would be excellent; he had already filled a hole in hers.

"It's up to you," he had said to her, "but I think you should go. Why stay home all alone when you can go to a party and enjoy yourself?"

So she decided to go, taking transit to the closest intersection, then walking the rest of the way. The music could be heard all the way down the street, mostly bass, turned up and throbbing like a heart. It started to rain and she was without an umbrella, so she ran. A little later, when she was standing in a crowd, chatting and sipping a rum and Coke, she felt two hands rest on her shoulders and heard a voice from behind. "Even soggy, you're a sight for sore eyes."

That night with Kevin was a fluke. Who would have thought they would run into each other at a party that Richard couldn't attend because he had to work? She and Kevin had been together several years earlier, the summer she was eighteen. No commitments; there were universities to attend and careers to secure. Kevin was heading off to an Ivy League college in the States to study business, while Anita had been accepted into the chemistry programs of three top local universities and had picked the one closest to home. Sex was something that had happened between them. It happened again, aided by memories and alcohol.

There was the baby to think about. She had been on antibiotics at the time, for an ear infection. A warning came with her birth control pills. She had read it only once in her teens when she first started taking the oral contraceptives. She considered an abortion, discussed the option with her doctor. He told her she needed to make a decision quickly, but she let the deadline pass. It wasn't that she was religious or that she thought it was wrong. Some days it seemed perfectly right; other days, not right for her.

The child could belong to either of them; both had similar features. Kevin was so excited when she told him. "We'll get married," he said. "I hope it's a girl."

Anita had weighed her options and made her decision. It was a decision she would consider every time she handed over her baby to the nanny that Kevin's mother offered to procure, and when she returned to university to get her master's debt-free. Later she would consider it again when her daughter walked down the aisle as flower girl at Judith's wedding and upon seeing a photo announcing that Richard had become Head of Cardiology at St. Michael's Hospital.

She would consider it every night for the rest of her life.
This was something she knew for a fact while standing
in the window watching the shoreline become obscure.

Thomas and the Woman

Thomas woke up on a Tuesday morning to find a woman in his house. She was standing at the counter in his narrow kitchen with a spatula in her hand, flipping pancakes in his electric frying pan. He nearly bumped into her, not being fully awake and, of course, not expecting a person, let alone a woman, to be blocking his path to the coffee maker. He couldn't entirely recall the previous evening to provide an explanation for her presence. His memory offered only vague glimpses of a barbeque with a horseshoe pit and chests of beer on ice. She gestured towards his table, squished against the wall at the far end, where there was a place set with a fork and knife, a mug of coffee and a glass of orange juice. Easing around her, he sat in his chair, picked up the glass of juice, and downed it in two gulps while she placed a plate in front of him stacked with several pancakes that appeared to have had thin wedges of apples pressed into them before they were flipped. He ate the way hungry men do, concentrating solely on the food and the travels of the fork from the plate to his lips. Afterwards, eyeing the woman over the rim of his coffee mug, he decided that it was good. It being the food and the preparation of the food and the woman standing in his kitchen.

She liked to do things. Clean windows. Make curtains. Hang pictures. She had two large photos of lilies, one with yellow flowers, one with orange, nicely matted and framed, and decided that one of these should hang in the front hall, on a particular wall that faced the entrance and was about four feet wide. She picked the yellow one, lilies the colour of sunshine, and centred the frame horizontally on the wall, placing it at eye level and holding it there with a hook and picture wire. Three little taps with a hammer, that was all it took. Then she stood back and looked, tilting her head, first to the left and then to the right, trying to decide if it worked. For three days, every time she walked past the yellow lilies, she stopped and looked. On the fourth day, she took them down and hung the orange lilies up in their place. The orange was crisper and more vivid, but again she hesitated every time she happened by. After two more days, she turned the picture from landscape to portrait, causing the three large blooms to form a triangle the shape of a female's pubic area. The largest flower, positioned on the bottom, was angled in a way that was both daring and inviting. Then she stood back, palms together in front of her with her fingertips resting on her chin, and nodded her head with approval because now she was sure that the photo called out for attention.

There was property, several acres, that went with Thomas's house. She decided to put in gardens, starting small at first, with a few plots of vegetables and some flowers and shrubs around the building's foundation. Slowly they grew, not just the flowers and vegetables but the actual size of the planted fields, until almost every square foot produced something. Something to harvest.

And harvest she did. She set up a market at the side of the road next to the house, and sold tomatoes, broccoli, lettuce, asparagus, kohlrabi, carrots, and beans. And bouquets of lilies and gladioli and mixtures of coneflowers and black-eyed Susans. In October, her pumpkins were much in demand. Come November and December, her preserves and wreaths and sprigs of holly became seasonal favourites.

When Thomas went to work, his co-workers would often approach him at the water cooler or the urinal to deliver compliments. "Her vegetables are some good," a co-worker would say, "had some with my supper last night and they were some good." Or someone else would say, "Took a drive out your way the other day, Thomas. It was our anniversary, and I had to pick up a bouquet of her flowers for my wife. They are considered second to none, ya know." Thomas would wipe his mouth with the back of his hand or fumble with his fly front before nodding and smiling with agreement.

He enjoyed this attention and upon returning to his desk would sit idle for several minutes, basking in the success of the woman's harvests.

Hummingbirds were attracted to her bee balm and monarchs to her milkweed. Other birds also found things to their liking, and soon, species considered rare for the area were stopping by while in migration. Bird-watchers and naturalists would pull over in their vehicles to scan the area from their car windows with binoculars in hand. The woman noticed this and, knowing that she had plenty of room to do so, created paths that curved their way through the various plantings to enable the enthusiasts better access. She edged them with stones and filled them with pea gravel, the tines of her rake making a musical sound as she spread the tiny pebbles that were delicate shades of pink, grey, blue, and taupe. She set up benches and enclosures the size of small bus shelters in case of rain, then added birdbaths and feeders and little hand-painted signs to identify plants and indicate points that might be of interest.

When people came to visit, they told their friends, who told more friends, and before long, there were lineups of vehicles on the shoulder of the highway. The municipality, recognizing that these people purchased gas and ate at local establishments, widened the shoulders, but they had a tendency to erode every winter so they built a parking lot on county land across the road. They placed two billboards advertising the property at each end of their jurisdiction and included it in all their tourist literature.

"Your property has become a destination, Thomas," one of his co-workers said one day while handing him an article snipped from a magazine. "Look at this. People are coming from all over the country to see it. Who would have thought?" Thomas glanced at the article and smiled, then pinned it up on the bulletin board next to his cubicle so everyone could see and comment on it. A large photo showed his house and the market and the acres that stretched out behind. An inset showed the author, no one he recognized, pointing and holding up a guidebook. The bulletin board became crowded with such articles. Sometimes co-workers would give them to him personally while making complimentary comments about the feature. Other times he would arrive at work to find another one added to the collection, the bright white of new paper catching his eye. When they told him his property was on the national news, Thomas was a little disappointed, as he always went to bed before the news, and he had nothing tangible to pin up on the bulletin board.

One day a man arrived. He walked the property in awe, delighted with every twist and turn of the path. "This…" he said, hesitating because he couldn't find the right words, "I could spend every day here. Do you mind if I help?" So the next morning he arrived, dressed in light clothes and a straw hat to cover the bald spot on his head, his body pale from the lack of sun. For days, he followed the woman around the property, watching her movements until he felt sure of what to do. Then he began on his own to weed and hoe and water and compost, not harvesting until verifying with the woman that her crop was ready. They worked acres apart and side by side, sometimes in silence, other times engaged in enthusiastic conversation. Soon, he looked like her, his arms and legs a maple-syrup brown, his muscles taut and shiny with sweat. But it was the expression on his face that had changed the most.

Soon others came, men and women who arrived every morning to stay for the day. Together they dug a small well and installed water features to erase the ever-increasing noise of traffic. They created evergreen hedges that encircled the property and hosted songbirds in both summer and winter. Thomas would arrive home from work just as these people were leaving. He would hear their bantering as he walked from the car to his front door. The man who had come first was always the last to leave. He would wave and smile at Thomas, and Thomas would smile and nod his head because his hands were full, carrying the newspaper and his keys and his briefcase and the lunchbox that the woman packed fresh for him every morning. Thomas liked the idea of these people enjoying the property, and the fact that they were helping to make it into a destination. But what he liked more were the meals that the woman would make for the two of them, the fruit and vegetables of the season prepared and served in their prime. Sometimes raw, sometimes cooked, they were nature's bounty at its best. He considered himself fortunate to be the recipient of such fine food.

It was on a Saturday morning that Thomas woke up to discover the woman gone. He searched the house, but found only her slippers under a stool in the kitchen and her bathrobe hanging on the back of the door. He continued to look for her outdoors, where he wandered the curved paths and planted rows of the property until he was overwhelmed. Never before had he fully explored the garden or understood the enormity of the accomplishment as a whole. Previously he might have considered a single tomato or a serving of beets to admire their healthy perfection and, while eating, savour their flavour. But this was different, something that was much greater than the sum of its parts. For hours he roamed the property, sometimes stopping to sit on a bench or observe a goldfinch busy at a feeder. He watched other birds, ones that he didn't recognize, eat red currants from a bush. And saw butterflies land on the flat surfaces of large petals and remain quiet and still for indeterminable lengths of time. He listened to the trickling of water running in streams that he hadn't known existed. At one juncture, he could smell peaches so strongly that his mouth watered. Around another bend, a scent of lavender that took him back to his childhood and his mother's dresser drawers. He wanted to share these revelations with the woman but found he had no words in his vocabulary to describe his feelings. He had never been a man who made speeches. Or a poet. Or a reader. He tried to remember if and when he had experienced similar emotions in the past, thinking that maybe, if she returned, he could explain with comparisons. Surely she must know already, but still he wanted to tell her how moving it all was. If, he thought, if she returned, suddenly aware that the word "if" was highly unreliable. His eyes watered and his breath caught in his throat as he choked back a sob.

He spent the whole day out on the property, finally but reluctantly groping his way back to the house when he could no longer see due to the absence of a moon. Stepping into the front hall, he switched on the light and looked up to see the picture of lilies on the small wall in front of him. The photo was faded from hanging every day in the path of the sun's rays that shone through the rectangular window of the door. The three washed-out blossoms of the triangular composition appeared to have once been a vibrant orange. He stared at them, tilting his head, first to the left and then to the right, and wondered how long they had been there.

Knowing

On a morning when half the bridge was missing, I dropped a token into the basket of the tollbooth and watched the light turn green. Drivers proceeding onto the span were required to take a leap of faith as they drove through the dense fog, trusting that they wouldn't encounter a severed end of asphalt and steel and plummet into the harbour below. Suppressing the urge to shift into reverse, I turned up the volume on the radio and sang while my wipers stuttered over flecks of moisture on the windshield and my feet, left on the clutch, right on the brake, pivoted on the heels of my shoes to move the car forward in a start-stop fashion.

Shortly after turning twenty-three and marking my one-year anniversary working at a jewellery store, I enrolled in the business program at the community college in Halifax, with much encouragement from my co-workers, anxious older women, who, like my mother, feared I lacked purpose. Copies of my application forms were tucked in a brown envelope under my purse on the passenger seat, along with the letter that notified me of my entry interview scheduled for 9:15. After crossing the bridge, I made a left on Gottingen, a right on Cornwallis and another left onto North Park, then continued to zigzag my way through the city streets until I pulled into the college parking lot at five past nine, just enough time to find a washroom and tame the frizz in my hair before I checked in.

The interview took place in a vacant classroom with chalk dust still heavy in the air. A panel of three people, two women and one man, sat across from me at a large table and asked questions while they reviewed my application and made additional notes. "Is there a specific reason why you want to take this course?" one of the women asked. She rested her chin on the back of one hand, and balanced a black pen like a cigarette between two fingers of the other while she waited for my answer.

"No," I replied. "I'm not sure what I intend to do once I complete the program, but I believe the skills I acquire will enable me to find a better job." This must have been close to what she wanted to hear because I was immediately accepted into the program.

On the first day of classes, I noticed a familiar face in the room, a pretty redhead who, although not a friend, was an acquaintance from high school. Both of us were from the Dartmouth side of the harbour, a situation that produced a similar bond to one created when two Canadians met while travelling Europe. Her name was Sheri. We quickly became allies, sitting next to each other in every course and developing a bit of a reputation for pushing the limits. We especially enjoyed flustering our accounting instructor, a small man who was not much more than five years our senior. This we turned into a competition to see how quickly our remarks would cause him to blush or remove his glasses and wipe the perspiration from his forehead. Of course, in the keeping of books, debits and credits line up in their proper places, columns are totalled, and numbers are either black or red; so no matter how disruptive we were, Sheri and I made excellent marks.

We attended the college dances, usually arriving in my beat-up car that occasionally left us stranded if the alternator went or the battery died. That's how we met Brian. He gave us a boost when the car refused to start after stalling at a light. It was late November, cold, windy and dark. We stood next to my brown and rusted Acadian, its flashing amber lights reflecting off the wet pavement, shivering while irate drivers pulled out around us, and giddy from the litre of wine we had finished while parked behind the Canadian Tire store.

He pulled up in an old Toyota that looked no better than my Acadian. "You ladies need some help?"

Ladies! Sheri and I made eye contact, then quickly looked away for fear we would burst into laughter and scare him off.

"I have cables," I said, the wine making my voice louder than usual.

"Good, I'll just turn around up here then."

Brian manoeuvred his car so that our front bumpers almost kissed. I popped the hood before retrieving the cables from the back hatch. He wiped the battery terminals with a rag that looked like it might have been a pyjama shirt several years earlier. As he attached the cables, I slipped in behind the steering wheel.

"We should invite him to the dance," Sheri said, leaning in the open window.

At the same moment, I heard Brian's okay and turned the key. The engine coughed a few times, so I pressed the accelerator and it started to idle. "Go for it," I said. "He's pretty easy on the eyes and he thinks we're ladies."

"Can I follow you ladies somewhere to make sure you arrive safely?" he asked.

There was that word again. It was difficult to stifle the urge to giggle.

"We're going to the dance at the college," said Sheri. "Would you like to come?"

He introduced himself and tagged along. When we arrived, we dragged three empty chairs up to a loud table at the back and sat down. Pint bottles slipped out of denim jackets to offer us sips of premixed drinks, and we settled into the wildness of the event. By the time the night was over, I had allowed myself to be picked up by a senior from the drafting program, and Brian, obviously smitten with Sheri, offered to drive her home.

After that, Sheri and Brian started seeing each other on a regular basis, while Sheri and I continued our day-to-day antics without interruption. She never really said much about him, other than that they'd gone to a particular movie or for a drive down the shore on the weekend. I would see him when she brought him to a dance, or when I met them somewhere for a drink.

Right before graduation, Sheri and I went out together for the last time. We went to The Villager, a Dartmouth pub known for live music and cheap draft. People filled the tables and crowded the bar. Most were our own age, or slightly older; many we recognized as regulars. Cigarette smoke coiled towards the ceiling like unfinished thoughts, while a cover of Bob Seger's "Night Moves" vibrated four-foot speakers. As usual, the dance floor was full. Within minutes of finding a seat, both of us were asked to dance.

"What's your opinion of Brian?" Sheri asked when we found ourselves back at our table together.

"I think he's nice, but I don't know him the way you do. Why?"

"He is nice, and my parents really like him. They think I should marry him."

"Do you want to marry him?"

She didn't answer me. She was asked to dance by one of the regulars and said yes to him instead. I sat watching her, how whenever she stepped under the blue spotlight, her hair turned crimson. Then a plaid shirt blocked her from my view. I looked up and smiled and was escorted to the floor. By the time we were together again, our mood was celebratory and the unfinished conversation was abandoned.

I didn't see much of Sheri after graduation. Both of us fell into routines that involved new jobs and different people. I wasn't surprised, several months later, when a wedding invitation arrived with her return address on it. Not until I opened it. She was marrying someone named Carleton Baker.

"I'm pregnant," she confided, looking slim and white on her wedding day.

"Well, you could have fooled me." We were in the kitchen of the reception hall. I was downing a glass of wine, and she was sipping ice water.

"We're both very excited," she continued, "and glad to be starting our family while still relatively young."

I had recognized Carleton from The Villager, had probably danced with him myself on numerous occasions. I was still wondering what had happened to Brian but thought it best not to ask too many questions.

A few years later, while walking on Granville Street, I ran into Brian. He greeted me with a large smile, and we decided to have lunch together. Holding pizza slices on paper plates, we strolled among the crowds of the busker festival taking place on the Halifax waterfront. A man with a diamond earring and dark hair tied back with a leather thong juggled torches of fire while standing on another man's shoulders. Afterwards we walked over to the Maritime Museum of the Atlantic and sat facing the harbour. Brian told me he worked for the provincial government, and I sheepishly had to admit that I was on my third job since finishing college.

At the time, I was sharing a house with two guys, one an electrician, and the other a carpenter. Both of them had a bit of a thing for me, and I had a bit of a thing for the carpenter, who had an on-again-off-again girlfriend. We were all blatantly obvious, although none of us made a move, preferring instead to exist playfully in the midst of the sexual tension. When Brian asked me out that afternoon, I accepted.

We began dating, neither of us mentioning Sheri or what had happened between them. On weekends, we liked going to bars where we could dance. Other times, we would either go to a movie or rent a video and watch it in his small basement apartment, on a sofa bed covered with a chevron afghan that was a nubby orange and green. When I stayed the night, Brian was always careful, using condoms even though I told him I was on the pill.

Mostly, we rented romantic comedies, forgettable paint-by-number stories of couples falling in and out and back in love again, stories that ended without a need to know what comes after. "You choose," Brian always said. Since I didn't care for violence or car chases, and movies requiring too much concentration had a tendency to put us to sleep, romantic comedies, as shallow as they were, were my preferred option. We must have watched hundreds of them by the night Brian started talking about marriage. It wasn't as if he was proposing, just prioritizing his dreams and stating a game plan. The apartment still smelled of the popcorn we'd made earlier. The credits rolled, and the movie theme played in the background. "I don't think I want to have kids until I can afford a house," he stated, turning the volume down on the television.

"How long do you think that will take?" I had the notion that Brian was feeling me out. Marriage and children were not things I had previously given much thought to. My sister had been the one who dressed up as a bride and played house with dolls and dishes. I was the one who bombed train cars with mud balls one day and imagined being a movie star the next. I slipped into the concept, picturing a sequined gown and four-inch heels, and allowed myself to get hung up on the details of the shoes before Brian responded.

"Another few years," he said. "That's why I live here, to save money. I already have a sizable down payment. I don't want to be a slave to a high mortgage, and my wife can stay home after the kids are born."

"But what if she wants to work?"

"She won't need to. My salary will cover everything. Don't you think it's better for the kids?"

I was holding a brown plastic bowl still half full of popcorn and set it on the coffee table. "But what if she *wants* to work?" I asked again.

He hesitated and appeared to struggle with the question. When he did respond, his voice was weary. "I would never expect her to stay at home if she really didn't want to. I was just thinking about having kids."

I carried the popcorn bowl to the sink and asked him to drive me home. He did and, as always, walked me to the front door. Then he leaned in to kiss me. What I did was involuntary. Something inside me had shifted, as if smelling an odour so vile that my stomach turned. Just as his lips touched mine I retched. There was the tightening in my throat and jerking motion of my head, which alone I could have probably explained. But the offensive noise that accompanied them could be nothing other than the sound of a gag. It was dark. I didn't see the look on his face when he pulled away from me and turned around. Neither one of us said a word.

I slept with the carpenter that night, maybe to convince myself that I was still desirable. I sought him out, offered him the bottle of Southern Comfort I grabbed from the fridge, and used my body as a chaser. In the morning, after vomiting any remnants of the syrupy liqueur left in my stomach, I told him not to ditch his girlfriend for me because I was leaving. I couldn't stay — the electrician would never forgive me.

Not only did I leave the house, I also left my job and the province. It seemed like a good thing to do at the time. I moved to Toronto, where I flitted between jobs. Then I attended university, where I flitted between majors until I couldn't afford to go anymore. I was working at a temp agency and living with an engineer when I decided to return home for a visit. The excuse was to see my parents. The actual purpose was to create some space so I could plan my eventual escape from

Toronto. Although I couldn't put my finger on precisely what it was I needed to get away from, I had to leave the city.

For the first weekend, I spent all my time with my mother and father. We visited my brother and sister and their families and ate out at an Italian restaurant that was the newest dining spot in Dartmouth. My mother said that the building used to be a gallery, and before that, it was a residence, one of the older homes in the area. It was moved up Main Street to its present location after the old property had been purchased to build a strip mall. I told her I had no recollection of the building or what was once in the spot where it now stood. "You were never one for such details," she said before gushing over the warm tones of the decor.

I wanted to ask her what she meant but decided not to, aware that she would turn it into something bigger than a discussion about an old house. All our telephone conversations carried the same undertone, as if she wanted to hear words other than those I delivered. "I'm thinking of moving back," I said to change the subject. "I was wondering if I could live at home for a bit until I got on my feet."

The two of them glanced at each other, passing a look between them before my mother responded. "Your father and I will certainly be happy to have you home, and we have no problem with you staying with us for a bit, but what about that guy you're living with? Where does he fit into all this?"

On Monday morning, after my parents went to work, I lounged in my housecoat, eating cold cereal and flipping through *The Chronicle Herald*. I don't normally read the business section, preferring the lighter fares of lifestyles and entertainment, but something caught my eye. A face in a photo on the section's front page, the woman projecting such confidence that the camera lens was able to capture it the way it captures sunlight or snow. It was Sheri, standing next to Carleton. I skimmed the article that summarized how they owned and operated the fastest-growing financial planning franchise in the city. It mentioned the many charities they supported and how they balanced their lives to afford their children, twelve and fifteen, the quality time they deserved. I don't know why it never dawned on me before. I'd always thought that what had happened to Sheri was unfortunate, not realizing until that moment that getting pregnant by Carleton, and I had no doubt it was by Carleton, was not an accident.

Several days later, I decided to put on my favourite outfit and go to the mall. I had purchased the floral red dress in a trendy boutique in Toronto, then splurged on matching shoes. I felt as though I was making a statement that flaunted my future independence. I enjoyed the turning of heads as I paraded through the corridors, my heels click-clicking on the tiled floors. I relished the idea of returning to live in the area.

After a brief snack at the food court, I went to The Bay and began rifling through sales racks. I heard a child laugh and looked up. Brian was there, corralling a rambunctious toddler. I had forgotten what a small place Halifax-Dartmouth could be, how easy it was to collide with the past. Next to him was a woman pushing a stroller draped with several garments to purchase or try on. The boy, a miniature version of Brian, giggled and veered between racks while his father gave chase. Neither of them noticed me. For an instant I was beset with an avalanche of emotions. Longing. Remorse. Claustrophobia. Then I quickly stepped out of their path and was about to turn away when the woman glanced up and caught my eye. On her face, I saw the look of someone who knew exactly what she was doing, staring at someone who never would.

Stepsister

In my mind, I pictured my father, large, in a red plaid shirt of wool — the stereotype uniform of all woodsmen — his orange hair and beard matted with sweat and crumbs of leaves. At least, that's how I thought of him as a child. I don't actually remember the colour of his hair. I was barely two when he disappeared, my sister only a baby. It is possible that he was the victim of a forest creature, mythic or otherwise. Perhaps a wolf swallowed him whole, like Red Riding Hood's grandmother. All he needed was to be set free. We waited years for him to return, until my mother moved us to the village and got a job at Frank Rella's pub.

Mother soon married Frank, who had a daughter of his own named Sydney. My sister Josephine and I took his last name, preferring it over ours, which was Smith. We moved into Frank's cottage, located on a cobblestone side street a couple blocks north of the pub, a nice neighbourhood of Tudor residences with fenced-in yards.

Frank was a sipper and would nurse the same mug of ale for an entire evening, saying that he preferred to keep his head clear to run the business and take care of his family. He loved being surrounded by adoring females and was never short on compliments — one of the reasons my mother fell in love with him.

We girls bonded instantly, calling ourselves the Rella sisters — Flo (short for Florence), Jo, and Syd. In appearance, we were as different as the herbs that grew in the back garden. I was tall, much too tall, and awkward, constantly bumping my head on chandeliers and archways when I would forget to duck. Syd was curvaceous and beautiful — eye candy, but with brains. As smart as she was, she never clued in to the fact that she was a head turner. Jo was the girl next door, always smiling, covered in freckles. If you looked close, you could see how they clustered together to form what appeared to be a heart-shaped birthmark on her right cheek.

We idolized the three musketeers, who frequented Frank's pub and were described as witty and handsome by our mother. Not allowed inside, we spied on them through the alley window by secretly venturing from our cottage after dark. Later, in our bedroom, we would strip down to our bloomers and have sword fights, using feather dusters for weapons, each of us taking a swooning shift as the maiden in distress, all of us preferring to brandish the dusters.

Mother worked in the pub alongside Frank. She was a big woman with a big laugh. The patrons enjoyed her sense of humour and loved her meat pies, which were the best in the land. Her list of secret ingredients included hot sauce and tarragon. News of these delicacies had travelled far and wide. The king himself, disguised as a peasant, visited The Glass Slipper Pub twice a year for one of my mother's meat pies, which she always served with apple chutney. She would recognize him by the ring on his left hand that doubled as his royal seal. No one could figure out whether he stupidly forgot to take it off, or deliberately left it on. Star-struck, my mother was unable to speak in his presence, denying him the anecdotes and jokes he would no doubt enjoy as part of the peasant experience. "Cheap bugger," she would say after he was gone. "He never leaves a tip."

Mother and Frank were generally at the pub, so Syd, Jo, and I did most of the household chores. Once a week we would get into our grubbies, our term for the tattered clothes we worked in, and clean the cottage from top to bottom.

It was a Tuesday, not too hot. A breeze travelled through open windows from east to west, carrying fresh air and the bustle of the street into our rooms. We placed shoes as stops against inside doors to keep them from slamming shut. I was busy sweeping cobwebs and picking bats and other vermin out of the thatched roof. Jo was sorting laundry in the upstairs hall, while Syd scoured the kitchen. To this day, I find it hard to believe that a rabid dog managed to get inside the house. Later we discovered that we had left the garden gate open when we returned from our wanderings the night before. At some point, we must have left the back door open as well. Syd shrieked when the creature crept out from behind the stove with strings of saliva hanging from its teeth. Then she panicked and ran, with the mangy dog following, out the front door and into the street. From my vantage point in the upstairs bedroom window, I saw the shocked looks on the faces of those who watched Syd sobbing in her threadbare clothes.

Things quickly became distorted, as things tend to when the rumour mill runs amok and the local papers only get half the facts. The next day's edition ran an engraved-plate image of Syd in her cleaning attire, along with a sensational headline and quotes from the neighbours about how wicked and abusive her step-relatives were.

Someone called Child Welfare. Their mediaeval representative made a surprise visit, only to find Syd dressed in a lovely peau-de-soie pinafore, her feet resting on a tasselled stool. She was reading — a pastime considered inappropriate for young girls of our time. They would have preferred her to be tatting lace or eating curds and whey. Mother was severely lectured for this, after which the ill-treatment-of-Syd matter was dropped. A retraction was printed on page eleven of the paper, a single paragraph lost in columns of jousting scores.

People looked at us differently after that. Unless Syd did the shopping, we received the worst cuts from the butcher and sour milk from the dairywoman's cows. Business at the pub slowed for a while but fortunately not for too long. The competition, a fast-food-ale joint lacking in decent cuisine and atmosphere and a seedy inn several kilometres out of town, didn't satisfy the hearts and stomachs of the local male population. They had stopped frequenting The Glass Slipper to appease their wives, then realized that the women didn't have the luxury of free time for drinking ale and eating meat pies and would never know they had returned.

Several weeks later, after most of the ruckus had died down, notices appeared, tacked to all the wooden doors in town, announcing a dinner and dance to be held at the castle. The parchment specifically stated that those arriving in business-casual attire would not be admitted.

We immediately dug into our trunks to retrieve our gowns, which were refashioned on an annual basis with new ribbons, silk flowers, glass beads or pearls. My gown required lengthening, as I had grown three inches since I'd last worn it. This, we decided, could be accomplished with a flounce. Jo was pleased to find that hers fit perfectly. It had been sloppy the previous year, constantly falling from her shoulders, so that she had to spend most of her time with her arms crossed or discreetly sliding the neckline back in place. Syd's curves got the better of her and proceeded to burst from the seams. The dress had been altered twice; no fabric remained hidden inside to let out.

Mother called every seamstress in town, only to be informed they were booked solid. How unusual, she thought, that not one of them was able to accommodate her. The household was in a state of panic. It's not as if a Gowns R Us outlet could be found in the market of our village. Then mother remembered Mrs. Godparent, wearily retired after thirty years of making gowns for primping, self-absorbed females. Promises of brandy and meat pies, as well as assurances that Syd was not the primping, self-absorbed type, secured her services.

By the afternoon of the event, Syd's dress had yet to be delivered. Mrs. Godparent sent a carrier pigeon with the message that she was running a few hours behind. There were no mice and no dramatic scenes where Jo and I tore apart a secretly constructed gown. I don't know how that silly rumour began.

"Go, go," Syd said, "or you'll miss the dinner. The food is always the best part. I'll catch up with you later."

The meal was over when Syd arrived. Most of the guests were outside on the patio, catching a breath of air while waiting for the musicians to begin playing. My sister was strategically positioned on top of a cartload of pumpkins, wildly driven by Mrs. Godparent. The old woman's silver hair had escaped from its usual bun and whipped around in a state of frenzy, sending dandruff flying in all directions that resembled fairy dust in the harvest moonlight. Through it all, Syd remained composed and beautiful. Jo and I watched, listening to the cooing of oohs and ahhs around us as though the fireworks had begun.

The prince, who had been exchanging pleasantries with a couple of dukes and the Duchess of Everafter, stood mesmerized, unable to move until Syd had gracefully climbed the stairs and curtsied apologetically before him. He had a slight lisp and kept pronouncing Sydney as Cindy. My sister was much too polite to correct him. They waltzed throughout the evening until Syd discovered she had to leave because she started her monthlies and had forgotten to slip some rags into her evening bag. Such explicit details could not be spoken to a prince. Instead she rushed past him, calling out, "I had a wonderful time, but I must go before it's too late."

Who is the mysterious Cindy? Syd, Jo and I, as naive as we were in thinking that it would all blow over, couldn't help but chuckle over the tabloid story and engraving that accompanied that headline. The entire town was buzzing. It's a small village. Everyone knows someone, and someone eventually directed the prince to The Glass Slipper, where he professed his undying love for the owner's daughter. A beaming Frank brought him home, forgetting that it was Sydney's day to clean the kitchen.

When the shocked prince proposed to a filthy Syd, it effectively placed her between a rock and a hard place. It is bad protocol to refuse a prince, and common knowledge that, in doing so, a girl would give the impression that she thought she was too good for one. I could tell Syd felt she had no choice. Under the circumstances and given the times we lived in, I would have probably done the same thing. I didn't get the chance to tell her, though. Sid was whisked away to the castle, for her own good, before we could speak again.

The second-last time I saw Syd was at her wedding. We did go to the wedding, relegated to the table of the town's assorted evil relatives. I was surprised to be in the company of so many and wondered if they were as bad as they were made out to be. Syd was almost in tears when she tracked us down. She said she had nothing to do with the seating plan. The queen had made all the arrangements, right down to choosing her pretentious wedding dress and ridiculous shoes. She lifted her dress to show us her feet, red with blood from where the crystal pumps were cutting into her skin. We searched our purses for hankies and mother gently padded them under the sharp edges.

After the wedding, the image of Syd in her tattered clothes appeared in the paper next to the official wedding engraving. The corresponding article served to propagandize the event as a valiant rescue of an ill-treated maiden by a noble, but perhaps starry-eyed, prince who could be forgiven any future transgressions.

A few months later, Jo reverted to Smith and took off with an artist who delighted in connecting the dots of her freckles to form constellations. The two of them run a travelling tattoo parlour. Her letters say she misses us but enjoys the anonymity of her lifestyle. Within two years, Mother died of a mysterious illness that I can only attribute to depression. She bequeathed to Frank her secret recipe.

There have been many times that I have thought about visiting Syd, just as I am sure that she has frequently thought about visiting me, both of us deterred by the fact that getting in and out of the castle alone is a bureaucratic and security nightmare that only a select few know how to navigate. I know her only through castle proclamations of births and visiting royalty. Poor Syd. I feel that she, stuck on the inside without an ally to escape with, as the three of us did when we braved the night to spy on the musketeers, is unable to navigate alone and spends her days treading water.

A few years ago I married Dwayne, the dragon master. He fell in love with me upon discovering that I could stand, look the creatures in the eye and they would allow me to wash behind their ears without breathing fire. He is a giant of a man and we are equally matched. Last week at our fundraising dragon wash, the proceeds going to the castle upkeep fund, since chivalry is now dead and tourist numbers are down, I saw Syd again. She was accompanying her children on an outing to see the dragons. She had miscarried four babies and laboured over five princesses before the obligatory prince was born. It is said that her husband no longer visits her at night. Frank often sees him at the pub. He doesn't hide his identity and he's not there for meat pies. Syd's father, and the only father I have ever really known, does not go in for gossip. If he makes a statement, it is true. It obviously pained him to make this one.

The dragons were uneasy with so many children about. Two things you can't trust together are dragons and children. Dwayne double-checked the cable fencing that kept the spectators at bay and filled buckets of water on standby. Sydney approached with my nieces and nephew, all holding white-gloved hands, from smallest to largest. From under the velvet of the girls' dresses came the rustling of crinolines and petticoats. Crystallized sunlight reflected from the tiaras in their hair and the jewelled buckles of the prince's shoes. When they stopped in front of the pen, the air was still, except for the occasional snort of a dragon. The crowd was silent. Waiting. Expecting.

I noted that Syd had acquired a couple of rolls around the middle. She took in the crow's feet that now radiate from the corners of my eyes and the chiselled lines at my mouth. I saw the edge of her lips twitch on one side as if she was about to break into a giggle, then her eyes moisten as if she was going to cry. We remained there, the thick wire of the pen between us, two women quietly acknowledging the fact that we were still sisters and friends, until the dragons and the children became restless.

Double Exposure

Why is it that you are always the last to know? It's two in the morning. You're thirty-six years old and you realize that your five-year relationship is in trouble. Your girlfriend stands before you in a short skirt and coordinating sleeveless tank with a low neck and a high midriff, moist as if returning from the gym, and tells you that you sometimes act like a mother. You tell her that she always acts like a child. Normally, you say that you are worried because she is unusually late. The argument is punctuated by broken glass, an exclamation mark, the smashing of your favourite photo, a cheesy picture of the two of you biting off the same slice of pizza. You used to think it reminded you of the Disney movie *Lady and the Tramp*. Perhaps Disney movies were the only things you ever really had in common.

You end the relationship, vowing to stay single because partnerships with other women are far too difficult for you to manage. You move into a new apartment, which you paint blue and yellow, then spend the next year immersed in your work while trying to adjust to being on your own again. You go to bed in men's boxers so you can slip your hand inside the fly front and indulge yourself when you have difficulty sleeping. Slip. Rub. Breathe. Moan. Sigh. Sleep.

At a New Year's Eve party, an acquaintance introduces you to a man who looks at you as if you are familiar. This man smiles and takes your arm to guide you to the kitchen, where he offers to open and pour the bottle of wine sticking out of your oversized purse. You are attracted to him and feel giddy inside, although you haven't dated men since high school. The two of you finish the wine and after midnight go to your place, where everything you once felt awkward about when around men now comes easy. He stays the night and you decide you could be convinced to change preferences. You spend the next day together, mostly in bed. He pleasures you with his tongue as women once did and you reciprocate. He tells you he is divorced and that his ex-wife is an artist. You tell him you're single and that you are a food photographer.

"Why food?" he asks.

"Because I don't cook," you reply.

He cooks, rummaging through your fridge and cupboards to find the ingredients for an impromptu fettuccine Alfredo while teasing you about your lack of domestication. You are stunned and amazed that he could produce something from almost nothing, the unused samples you bring home from the job. In a cupboard above the stove, he finds an unopened bottle of Jamaican Rum, a gift your brother brought home from vacation several years ago, and makes hot chocolate liqueurs for dessert.

On your second date with this man, you meet downtown. The snow is noisy, like corrugated cardboard breaking underfoot, so you walk without words to the Italian restaurant next to the farmers' market. The restaurant is empty, other than the two of you, and commands quiet, so you talk in whispers. He tells you he has an eleven-year-old daughter who stays with him some weekends. "Don't worry, she's a great kid," he says, before relating the details of her aquatic and music skills.

Afterwards, you spend the night at his place and he serves you an omelet filled with ham and cheese and fresh vegetables for breakfast. This man is a history professor at the university. He lives in a nineteenth-century house in the south end, the type of house portrayed in nostalgic paintings or Christmas movies — the epitome of security and happiness. He has silver strands of hair at his temples and discerning taste. He tells you that he, like most of his favourite people throughout history, has an affinity for beautiful women. You are conscious that he is trying to win you over with his charm and kitchen skills.

The first time you meet his daughter is at Swiss Chalet. "Kid food," the man says, deliberate neutral ground. When he leaves to use the washroom, she spits in your face and says she hates you and that you are not her mother. You wipe the spit off on the red logo of your napkin and tell her you are not trying to be her mother but would like to be her friend if that's okay. She doesn't smile but says that maybe it is. When the man returns, the two of you pretend nothing happened. She snatches glances at you over her half-full Shirley Temple. You don't know whether she is daring you to tell or imploring your silence.

In the summer, the man suggests that you give up your apartment and move in with him. You remind him again that you don't cook and he laughs and says he'll help you pack. In a box of things he is clearing away to make room for your stuff, you discover a photo of his ex-wife and notice that you both wear your blonde hair in a shoulder-length bob with bangs, and have brown eyes, and freckles across the bridges of your respective noses. "I think we look somewhat alike," you say, holding the picture up next to your face. Smiling, he takes the frame out of your hand and leads you to his study, where he undresses you and, on an antique armchair with eagle-claw casters, he reminds you why you decided to move in.

When this man goes to a conference, he asks you to allow his daughter to still come for the weekend. You do, and plan all kinds of things to fill the time. Shopping. Crafts. Disney movies. Making cookies with Pillsbury dough. On Sunday evening, you drive the daughter home. A blue SUV is in the driveway, curtains move, and a lamp is on upstairs. No one answers the doorbell. You bring her back to the house and try phoning, calling every fifteen minutes for several hours before her mother picks up. She tells you she was away, adds something about car trouble and being out of cellular range.

"She was lying," you tell the man.

"It happens," he says. "There is nothing I can do about it."

You feel angry with him and sorry for him at the same time.

Sometime in September, you run into your former girlfriend at a coffee shop. She looks fabulous, flirts with you and invites you to lunch. You are flattered and accept, then spend the morning torn and unable to concentrate on the compositions of cuisine you are trying to photograph. Lunch is at a new bistro overlooking the water. You are disconcerted and feel somewhat out of touch. You used to know whenever a new place opened in town. How had you managed to miss this one? What else have you missed?

You both order orange-almond salads and seafood crêpes. "I'm moving to Vancouver," she says, nibbling a breadstick. "Did I mention how much I still miss you?" Then she hesitates and lowers her voice. "Us. I miss us…what we had."

The conversation is mostly memories. Afterwards, she invites you back to the old apartment one last time.

Sex with this woman is as good as it always was, as good as with the man. You are empowered by your body, believe that it is you who is in control, not her or him, you and your attitude. You think you are freer than you have ever felt in your life. At home that night, you try things with the man you have never done with anyone before.

For his birthday, you go online and order toys — mischievous things (nothing too deviant) — that arrive by mail in discreet packages. "Want to play?" you say, raising your eyebrows, when he opens the gift.

"Pick a room," he replies.

Later you are surprised by the familiar skill with which he handles these things. He tells you it's been several years since he has enjoyed a woman like this, since sometime before his daughter was born.

"Well, then, it's been way too long," you say. "Happy birthday."

This man decides to write a book, a historical novel requiring passion and time-consuming research. You fall asleep to the sound of his fingers tapping the computer keyboard. You listen as he reads you his latest draft. His writing is good. Very good. When it is published, the launch party is held in the faculty lounge of the university. The room has the tallest windows you have ever seen in your life. Indeterminable yards of plush fabric hang in the guise of heavy draperies.

The man has many friends. They pull him in all directions, so you amble slowly around the room, admiring the pictures and the food. Somewhere between the canapés and the fruit tray, you are approached by one of his colleagues.

"Kathleen," he says, leaning forward and kissing your cheek, "so nice to see you again."

He smells like breath mints and aftershave. "Not Kathleen," you say, "Joan."

For a moment, he looks horrified, then regains his composure and offers a toothy smile. "My apologies," he says. "For such a crass error, I should at least get you another drink."

"Why not?" you say, handing him your empty glass.

While he makes his way to the bar, you seek out the man with your eyes, find him in a circle of people standing next to a table of books. He sees you and waves. The eyes of the circle turn to take you in and you smile and wave back.

"How long?" the colleague asks, arriving with a refill of red wine.

"At least four years," you reply.

"Sorry," he says again. "I honestly didn't know."

When she is fifteen, his daughter runs away from home and shows up at her father's (and your) place. He tells her she can stay, and calls her mother. During her first week, she skips school and misses dinner three days out of five. The man refuses to discuss the matter, afraid to scold her for fear she will run away again. It happens several more times before you take it upon yourself to rectify the situation. You offer her a job as your assistant after school and on weekends and to pay her for her time. It's conditional, you say, on her attendance in school, but you could really use the help.

While this man works on his second novel, you convince his daughter to continue her swimming and arrange for coaches. You spend time driving her to and from practice and to and from friends' houses, getting to know other parents on a first-name basis. Some of them become friends that you organize carpools with and meet for lunch.

You take pictures of them, this man and his daughter, tonal black and whites that you hang, in pewter frames with charcoal mats, on the walls of the upstairs hall. One of these will appear on the man's website and grace the dust jacket of his future novel. Sometimes, when he is typing at night, you let your hands roam down between your legs, arch your back, curl your toes, and hold your moans and sighs behind closed lips.

One afternoon, you arrive home to find the daughter crying. Her pillows and bedspread are drenched. Tissues are tossed about like carnations after a storm. She confides in you, tells you that she has missed her period. "Don't tell Daddy," she begs.

So you hold her and insist that everything will be fine. "Don't worry," you say. "We can manage this."

You make some phone calls, book a flight, plan a short trip. "Shopping" you tell the man, "a girls' vacation." Yes, it's okay if she misses school.

You fly in the day before to make mandatory purchases, high-end fashions at obscure boutiques. Some props for show and tell. The next morning, at the hospital, you tell them you're the girl's mother but kept your own name. After signing forms and producing valid ID, you follow her as far as allowed, then sit and worry. The waiting room is green, the only shade of green people find depressing. You flip through magazines that are three years old, trying to find something worth reading, then root through your purse for your cell phone and look through your contacts. You keep scrolling and scrolling and scrolling through the names, releasing bleeps with every touch of the button, until the nurse informs you that cell phones are not allowed in the hospital. When it's over, his daughter wakes, groggy and pale, and asks how soon she can return to swimming. At home, you explain to the man that she has the flu and must miss a couple more days.

Crossing the harbour on the ferry, you see the man's ex-wife with another woman. They are standing at the side rail. You watch, unable to look away, from the corner of your eye like everyone else, as the two women hold hands and exchange kisses. When they disembark, you want to follow, perhaps rake the ex over the coals, accuse her of being an irresponsible parent. Maybe. Or is it to get a better glimpse of the other woman? A fluttering sensation travels between your navel and your thighs. Your body feels like it is naked in a round room constructed of feathers and breezes that blow inward and tease your skin. Turning towards the parking lot, you hit the remote to locate your car while they disappear down a side street before you have a chance to notice which one. That evening, you suggest to the man that the three of you go out to dinner. "My treat," you say.

"What did I do to deserve this?" he asks.

"Cook," you reply.

After his daughter leaves for university, you and this man fall into the habits of a comfortable middle-aged couple. He writes, while you read until you fall asleep most weeknights. The two of you have dinner with friends on Fridays and take walks in the park on Sunday afternoons, have sex, once, maybe twice, a month. The very life people would attribute to such a nineteenth-century residence, the tasteful home of a photographer and a successful author. Circumstances you would never have imagined settling into when you were younger but now can't imagine being without.

When the daughter announces her engagement to an English playwright, you help her plan her wedding, including offering caterers from your list of clients. You pick up invitations and stick countless stamps on envelopes. The man walks her down the aisle and you admire the two of them. He is still handsome and charming but now radiates something else. Self-fulfillment, you think. She is a beautiful, happy woman with noteworthy accomplishments and future goals, a testament to your diligence.

At the reception, you are talking to the playwright about his latest work, commenting on his witty dialogue. "Your characters poke fun at their own foibles without knowing they are doing so," you say. "In any other circumstances, such naivety would give rise to pity."

"Yes," he agrees. "How perceptive of you to notice. It's amazing how many people don't."

You find him charming and think the daughter has married a man much like her father.

"Do you happen to cook?" you ask.

"We both do," he replies.

Across the room, you notice this man and his daughter sharing a laugh with his ex-wife, her mother. The woman has a presence. People hover around her like electrons. Someone wants a picture and the three arrange themselves for the camera. You look at the composition, the father on the right, the daughter on the left, both with their arms around the free-spirited-mother-ex-wife-artist in the middle. That's when it begins, the feeling of being faded, overexposed, and no matter how hard you try, you can't seem to shake it.

Autumn Trip East

Diane tilted her head downwards and glanced over her sunglasses to check whether they were exaggerating the autumn colours. She did the same thing every time she saw a tree that looked bright red or neon orange, or a cluster of hues so intense that she thought they couldn't be real. She had forgotten how beautiful fall was out east. The quantity and variety of trees made the difference, and the lack of industry and dust. The drive through Ontario and a large part of Quebec had been uninspiring. It wasn't until east of Quebec City, nearing Rivière-du-Loup, where nature began to hug the edges of the highway, that the season surrounded her, providing a spectacular show before the day turned dark, offering her something to look forward to in the morning.

Yesterday she had left Toronto and driven to Edmundston, stopping only to grab a bite at a cafe in Drummondville. It was possible to complete the trip non-stop if she drove all night, especially with the newly widened highways through New Brunswick. But Diane was not in a hurry, and Edmundston had always been the halfway point whenever she drove down with Blaine, or with him and the boys. This was the first time she'd travelled east on her own in over twenty years. Twenty-four, to be exact, she reminded herself. The divorce papers confirmed the fact. The last time she'd driven east was two years ago, right after she and Blaine had separated. The boys were with her. She and Liam had made plans to take the trip before Liam headed to university in the fall. Then Sheldon showed up, out of the blue, which was always his way, and they begged him to join them. They were surprised when he said yes. They had made the drive into a real vacation, taking several days and detouring to stop at all the tourist destinations that they usually skipped, staying only two days with her parents, then driving back through the States to do more sightseeing. Although Sheldon was quiet for most of the time, both she and Liam were glad he was there. It was the last time that the three of them had been together. Sheldon left again the day after they arrived home.

The border was ahead, easily identified by the hydro and radio towers that skirted the marsh between the ocean and the highway on the isthmus that tacked Nova Scotia to the rest of the country. The place where the map ended in her grade-four drawings, the ones that always had Cape Breton looking like a lobster claw on one side. She pushed the power button on the radio and was greeted with static, then hit the seek arrow in search of a local station. Rap, heavy and disquieting, filled the car. She touched the button again and heard The Eagles singing "Take It Easy," like a piece of sound advice from the past. It was easy to get seduced by the classic rock, which to most people her age represented some sort of idyllic youth, somewhere between angst and responsibility. Diane didn't want memories to sing along with, or lyrics to get stuck in her head for days. She just wanted a presence. She pushed the button once more and landed on a call-in show, advice for genealogy buffs on the CBC. She let it stay as she cruised by the Welcome to Nova Scotia sign.

Several kilometres past the border, she encountered a row of pylons. A flashing amber arrow directed vehicles into a single lane, and Diane geared down. After the traffic merged, she found herself inching along between two tractor-trailers that roared and groaned and smoked like dragons being pressed into service against their will. For twenty minutes she moved in this fashion, her feet, adept from years of Toronto congestion, automatically finding the perfect balance between stop and go.

She wondered about Sheldon. Was he hitchhiking or hopping trains? She knew he had done both in the past. Thoughts of Sheldon were never far from her mind, always lying in wait just below the surface of everything else. He had been gone seven months this time. She still scrolled through the history on her cell phone every couple of days, thinking that perhaps she had missed an incoming call that could have been her son. It was a habit that both she and Liam had acquired over the last few years. Not that Sheldon owned a phone, but every time he came home, Diane made a point of writing their numbers down for him. Afterwards, she would watch him fold the piece of paper in half and in half again and tuck it into the pocket of his jeans. Now that Liam was in university, Diane called him whenever Sheldon arrived, then left the room while he talked to his younger brother. Where Sheldon was concerned, Diane and Liam had a similar approach. When he came home, they were relieved and happy to see him. They tried to show him how much they loved him, hoping that it would make him stay. Blaine, on the other hand, was always frustrated. He wanted answers to questions that he was afraid to ask. He wanted everything to be fixed, to be their old definition of normal. Even when Sheldon wasn't there, Blaine could no longer move about the house without slamming and banging things.

The highway opened up again, and Diane signalled and pulled out around the rig in front of her. The truck let out a disgruntled snort as she accelerated past, and she held her breath against the odour of spent diesel fuel while glancing up to watch the vehicle shrink in her rear-view mirror. From here, she was pulled along by the familiar and before long was exiting the highway, preparing to merge onto Main Street. This was a part of Dartmouth that was seedy and resisted change. Diane took in the pavement in need of repair. The strip club, located just a couple of buildings away from the music store and conservatory where countless numbers of children were deposited daily for lessons. The tavern with another new name. McDonald's and the Dairy Queen. The empty lot with a truck selling mackerel. The lot had been vacant since Diane was a child. Vacant yet not, because there was always someone parked there selling something.

When she heard the siren, Diane glanced down to see that she had been doing sixty-eight in a fifty-kilometre zone. She pulled over across from an old church that was now a karate studio and watched in the side mirror as the police officer parked and got out of his car. Vehicles slowed and detoured around them; drivers checked her Ontario licence plates then offered a serves-you-right look. Diane turned off the radio and put down the window.

"Licence and registration please, ma'am."

Ma'am. The word made her cringe. "Right," she said, retrieving her licence from her wallet and her registration from the glove compartment. She handed them out the window and scrutinized the officer for the first time.

His face took her back. It was almost the same as it had been when she'd last seen him, but filled out enough to erase the scrawny features of a teenager. Contrasting with his ruddy tan, the few wrinkles visible on his forehead and around his eyes looked like fine lines drawn in chalk. They reminded her of how he used to squint whenever he was concentrating hard on something. Ethan had aged well. He didn't appear to recognize her, but then why would he? Her hair was now blonde and she wore contacts and had gained about thirty pounds. She had also changed her name when she married. There was absolutely nothing left to tie her to the kid who'd sat across the aisle from him in grade twelve English. She wrestled with the idea of saying hello and identifying herself, perhaps arranging to meet him later.

When he took her papers, she noticed his wedding ring. A plain gold band, scratched and worn and looking as if he had never taken it off. Well, at least he's not alone, she thought, not single for life as she had imagined him being so many times. *No use stirring up lumps in old porridge.* Her grandmother's saying. Diane could almost hear the old woman's voice dispensing words of wisdom between sips of brandy-laced coffee.

"So what brings ya to this part of the country?" Ethan was studying her licence. Along with a slight twang, there was an air of confidence in his voice that hadn't been there in his youth.

"Just visiting," Diane said, relieved that she had picked up a different dialect over the years.

"How long are ya planning on staying?"

He stared at her with a look that she couldn't decipher. She shifted in her seat and pressed her back into the lumbar support. "A week, maybe a little more."

"Enjoy your visit," he said, handing back her papers, "and do me a favour, slow down."

"Thanks. I'll do that! Not enjoy the visit. Well, yes, I'll try to enjoy the visit too, but I meant I'll slow down." God, she thought, I sound like an idiot. "What I'm trying to say is that I really appreciate this, and I'll be more careful."

"That's all I ask," he said, then turned and walked back to his cruiser.

Pulling into traffic, Diane considered what would have happened if, instead of babbling, she had let *Ethan* casually fall into place after *thanks. Thanks, Ethan.*

Diane parked on her parents' street and sat studying the details of everything in view. The houses were mostly small bungalows. One had been renovated to add a sunroom and larger kitchen. Another had ventured upwards to create an entire new floor, but most had remained the same for forty years, with the exception of new windows or siding to cover the original cedar shakes. After several minutes she reached for the keys and her purse and opened the car door. Traffic noise from Main Street filtered through the yards. Starlings jostled and bickered on the hedge. Somewhere there were wind chimes, the kind made of various lengths of pipe. The kind that clanged instead of tinkling.

"Diane!" Her father opened the door with a broad-faced grin and scooped her into a hug. "What on earth are you doing here, girl?"

"Just felt like coming for a visit." She nestled her face into his shoulder and inhaled the familiar smells of his shampoo and shaving cream, along with something new. Body wash. One of those clean, manly, almost sexy scents that made her think of an athlete in street clothes; certainly not one that she would have ever associated with her father.

"How long are you staying?"

"Maybe a week, I don't know for sure." She let him usher her inside, then stepped back to survey his appearance. "So, how come the door was locked?"

"Oh, you know how it is," he said, trying to disguise the look of helplessness that had momentarily appeared on his face. "Can't trust anyone these days. And with them always letting people out of the Burnside jail by mistake, a person doesn't feel safe in their own home."

The toilet flushed and her mother stepped into the hallway, closing the bathroom door behind her. "Too many people in that jail, and too few guards. That's what they say, anyway. Shouldn't have jails so close to communities, in my opinion. Did I hear you say you were staying for a week?"

Doris never changed. Her dyed hair and pencilled eyebrows had been part of her public persona for as long as Diane could remember. That and a brusque demeanour that Diane suspected her mother no longer dropped for her father, like she used to when they were younger and in bed and Diane could hear them through the adjoining wall.

"Something like that. Hope you don't mind that I didn't call?"

"We'll have to get some groceries, that's all. We don't keep a lot in when it's just the two of us. I see you came on your own. Surely one of the boys could have driven down with you."

"Liam is in university. And Sheldon couldn't make it either." Diane couldn't bring herself to say that Sheldon had disappeared. She hadn't told them when he had disappeared the first time, when he was fifteen and she and Blaine hardly slept for three months. That time, he had left a note. *Mom, Dad, I'm just going away. Don't worry.* It was the only time that he had left a note. Every time after, he was just gone. She never told them.

"Well, get yourself settled in. Your father and I will make a trip to Sobeys. Find your keys, Bill. I'll get my purse."

Diane unpacked the charger and plugged in her cell phone. Then she wandered through the rooms, all dark from blind slats angled partially closed under her mother's mandatory three-to-one ratio of gathered sheers and half-drawn insulated drapes. She returned to her own room to push back the curtains and raise the blinds. Opening the window and leaning on the sill, she peered out, searching the far corners of the backyard to pick out the mock orange and snowball bushes she had helped her father plant the summer she turned eight. Towering between them was the variegated maple. Somewhere, she recalled, there was a photo of Liam and Sheldon eating hot dogs while sitting in its branches, their bare legs dangling just out of her reach.

"I bought a turkey," her mother said when they returned. She was carrying two Sobeys bags, reusable green totes with pictures of enlarged blueberries on the side. Her father followed with two more bags. These ones had pictures of artichokes on them.

"Mom, I really don't want you to go to a lot of trouble." Even as she said it, Diane knew that things were already in motion and picking up speed.

"Nonsense, everyone was coming next weekend for Thanksgiving anyway. We're just moving the date up."

For the rest of the afternoon, her mother bustled happily around the kitchen with an upgraded sense of purpose. Diane and her father donned sweatshirts and sat on the deck drinking beer. For dinner, Diane talked them into ordering takeout by insisting that she was craving a donair. Her parents preferred pizza, so she picked up a medium with everything except black olives for them. While she was out, she rented a movie, a family flick with a kid and a dog. By ten-thirty, they were all in bed.

It was after eleven when she strolled into the kitchen the following morning. Her mother was already filling the turkey with handfuls of stuffing.

"What can I do to help?"

"Get yourself some breakfast, then start the vegetables. We'll all be wanting to shower later, so we need to do the dirty work first."

Diane put the leftover pizza in the microwave and poured herself a glass of milk.

"You're eating like a teenager," her mother said.

"No, I'm not. If I were a teenager, I would drink from the carton."

"You wouldn't be eating like that if the boys were around."

Actually, thought Diane, I probably would be. After Sheldon started disappearing, she began reevaluating everything. When he was home, if he wanted to eat potato chips and ice cream sundaes for breakfast, she didn't say a word. Often, she joined him, stealing a few minutes of his time while coveting more. She bought junk food and took up baking again, deliberately leaving things where he would see them, another one of her desperate ideas. The sad fact was that Sheldon wasn't much of an eater. When he did eat, he was silent and picked at his food, and she studied his hands and thought about how much they were aging and of all the things they probably did to survive when he wasn't at home. They were scarred and usually bruised. Concentrating on them kept her from imagining some of the other things he could possibly do for food or money.

Everyone arrived just after five. Doris hustled them all into the dining room and began placing platters of food on towels, folded in quarters, in the middle of the table. Diane took the seat next to Julie and Allison, her nieces, while Barry and his wife, Caroline, sat on the other side and her parents took their usual spots on the ends.

"The dishes are hot," her mother said. "Diane, you scoop the potatoes since they are in front of you. The girls can serve the squash. Caroline, you do the asparagus, and I'll manage the dressing. There is a platter of turkey at each end, and we'll pass around the gravy and cranberries." Doris belonged to an era where such tasks were women's work. Holiday dinners meant that all the women, whether they were guests or not, were also expected to be in the kitchen afterwards. The men were allowed to smoke, drink or fall asleep.

Diane had resented this in her teen years, but then did the same with her own sons, always wanting to do things for them, never expecting them to help out. On the other hand, she never expected help from other women either. Blaine always pitched in. It was one of the reasons she had married him. The only one she could remember, but the memory was vivid. The first time was when she was still at York University. They had only been dating a short time when he invited her to his house for Sunday dinner. It was so nice to get out of residence and eat a real meal in a real house. Diane almost fell out of her chair when Blaine stood up, without being asked, and started clearing the table. She could hardly contain her astonishment when he washed all the dishes that didn't fit in the dishwasher while his father dried them. She wondered whether there were any men in Nova Scotia who would do that.

"So, how's the car business?" she asked Barry, piling his plate high with mashed potatoes.

"A bit slow, but there's always someone out there who wants to buy a truck. Prices are good these days, and even with gas being unpredictable, they can't resist."

"Sell many hybrids?" She handed him his plate and watched as he doused everything in gravy until his dinner looked like islands in a mud puddle.

"We don't even discuss hybrids unless someone is specifically looking for one. Then it's a special order."

"The boys will have to change their ways eventually."

"The boys," Barry said, holding his fork like a pointer in midair, "have been my livelihood for over twenty years. Don't expect me to start telling them what to do."

"Did I tell you about Eva Gibbons?" Doris said before Diane could respond. Diane had wanted to say something along the lines of everyone needing to change, that the only way to survive was to adapt. She took her cue and remained silent.

"Her husband Rob woke up to find her dead in the bed next to him. That was a couple months ago. An aneurysm. It's so sad to see him getting groceries all by himself now. You remember Rob and Eva. You used to babysit for them years ago."

"I only babysat for them once, but yes, I remember them."

"Allison, how's that floor hockey team of yours?" Her father's jovial voice came from the other end of the table. Diane looked up to see him wink at his granddaughter.

"We're going to the provincials, Gramps. You'll have to come watch." Allison was a feminine version of Diane's brother. She had his mouth and nose, and those damn long lashes that Diane always thought were such a waste on Barry. She had also inherited his athletic talents.

"Thought I'd get a van from work," Barry said. "Then we could all go to the games. Get a couple of hotel rooms if necessary."

"Sounds like a plan," said her father.

"So, Julie, are you on any teams?" Diane lifted her glass to take a sip of water but set it back down after catching a whiff of chlorine.

"I'm afraid that Julie takes after me," said Caroline. "Not much of an athlete, but she is in vocals and band."

"And I'm performing in the dinner theatre."

"Oh, wow! When's the dinner theatre?"

"Christmas," said Julie, "right before our semi."

"What on earth is a semi?" Doris said. "Sounds like a truck."

"It's a dance, Gran. You know, semiformal." Julie laughed, and Diane could picture her easily fitting in with any group of carefree girls making s'mores at a sleepover.

"I didn't know they had a dance at Christmas," said Doris. "I thought the only dress-up event was the prom at the end of the year. It's so nice that you kids like to do that sort of thing. Diane never went to her prom. Wasn't much for boys or going out back then. She was asked, though. Remember, Bill? Remember that poor bugger who showed up at our door all dressed up with a corsage in hand? Diane never even told us she was invited. Why anyone would just disappear instead of going, or at least telling the guy she wasn't going to go, is beyond me. Now in my day, I loved getting all gussied up in satin and rhinestones. Had the boys falling all over me when I went to prom. Not Diane. She just took off. Didn't come back for two days. Worried sick, we were. We called the police and they organized a search, then Diane shows up with the old pup tent we used to have in the garage." Doris shifted her gaze towards her daughter. "Wasn't that boy one of the Milligans? Ethan, wasn't that his name? Whatever happened to him?"

"He's a police officer," Caroline interjected. "His daughter is in Allison's class."

"A police officer," Doris said. She clicked her tongue and helped herself to a large slice of turkey breast. "You wouldn't have thought he had it in him. Not if you saw him on our doorstep back then."

After dinner, Diane and Caroline were filling plastic containers with leftovers and stacking them in the fridge. "So, what are you doing tomorrow?" Caroline asked, snapping the lid on a bowl of gravy.

Diane didn't hear the question. She was busy thinking of Sheldon, and of his need to turn destinations into departure points, and of the excuses she would make in order to leave before the week was up. She wondered whether she was becoming like her son or if he had been like her all along. Years later, long after Sheldon had disappeared for good and Diane only travelled when Liam picked her up from the seniors' home every other Sunday, she would still find herself pondering this more often than not.

Chasing Rabbits

The dog was off again. Jake could hear him racing through the weeds in Eugene's yard, heavy panting mixed with the hissing of disturbed vegetation. "Einstein!" he called, directing his voice through the thicket of black spruce that separated the two properties.

"Not too bright, that Einstein. Doesn't look like he's gonna listen."

The last thing Jake needed was Gene's sarcasm. For eight years, Einstein had never left the yard. Then Eugene added pet rabbits to the equation, minus a cage. For the kids, he said, but the kids moved out west with their mother after the divorce last year. The rabbits couldn't make the trip.

Originally there were three of them: two grey, one tan. Sometime over the winter, one of the grey ones disappeared. Must have been a hawk or an owl. It happened in Jake's driveway. Nothing left but red snow and bits of downy fluff. Whatever had gotten the rabbit, Jake kept hoping it would come back for another meal. He was getting tired of chasing the little bastards out of Maxine's gardens.

"That dog of yours gets a hold of one of my rabbits, I'll shoot him," Gene yelled.

Jake couldn't see him, but he had a pretty good idea where Gene was. When he was home, Gene was only ever in two places: in the front yard working on some wreck, or on the back deck downing a beer. Deck, concluded Jake, steering left and cutting through the trees to Gene's yard. He took the time to brush spider webs from his face and hair before clapping his hands, mostly for effect. There was no way in hell the dog was going to stop until he was tired, and no way he would catch a rabbit either, not with arthritis in his hip.

Gene was leaning on the deck rail, absently peeling the label off a beer bottle and wearing a look that Jake labelled as antagonistic pleasure.

Jake sidestepped a discarded tire rim. "What do you expect? He's a spaniel. It's only natural for him to chase rabbits. I never thought he would actually get the opportunity or I would have included it in his training."

"Like I said, he better not get one of my rabbits."

At the very least, Jake wanted to tell Gene to put a cork in it. It was either that or the litany of expletives that remained on the tip of his tongue when Einstein chose that moment to end the chase and come romping towards his master, tail wagging full tilt and looking as though he was expecting a reward. Jake slipped his hand under the dog's collar and retraced his steps to his own yard.

Einstein wasn't happy being kept in his pen. Jake didn't care. He had things to do; running after a dog was not one of them. First, he had to shovel the pellets of rabbit crap off the lawn so he could mow, then he was planning on weeding the gardens. Why Maxine had to have so many gardens was beyond him, and how she managed to keep them looking perfect was another mystery. At least once a week Jake thought about filling them in with sod. A few days ago, he went as far as taking the measurements of the two larger ones out back before changing his mind. Maybe he ought to just sell the place and move into town.

By the following week, the weather had changed. The air held the beginning of tropical storm season. Ever since the hurricane a few years back, this time of year made people uneasy. Jake strolled around the lawn, picking up branches that had come down in the previous night's wind. "Damn rabbits," he muttered, bending down to inspect the lower limbs on the lilac bush. He'd have to protect it with fencing, meaning a trip to Home Hardware. Jake, no different than any other male he knew, didn't mind going to the hardware store, but this time he minded the purpose.

The CD player in his truck played a single disk, *The Guess Who,* over and over in a constant loop. Randy Bachman and Burton Cummings. Jake knew all their lyrics. Nowadays, he just tapped his fingers on the steering wheel, but when he was younger, he would imitate them, singing their vocals, using a beer bottle as a mike. That's how he met Maxine, at a party, while singing "American Woman." She shimmied up to him and asked what he thought of Canadian women. He could still see her in those slim-fitting Levis and purple halter. She even had purple shoes. It was the first time Jake saw someone wearing shoes that weren't black, white, or some shade of brown. God, she looked good. He always wondered what she saw in a goofball like him. Both only children, they didn't bother to have kids of their own. Lots of people opt not to have kids these days. Back then it was a bit of an issue. Their parents never understood that it was a choice; never forgave them, either.

Maxine always said that the plaza had everything you needed for a summer weekend. As long as you don't need a new bathing suit. Then she would laugh. What had started as a lone grocery store had expanded over the years to include the hardware store, a liquor store, a pharmacy and a Tim Hortons. The parking lot, already too small before Tim's moved in, was busy. Twice Jake had to slam on his brakes to avoid hitting someone attempting to back out of a spot. He pulled his truck in on an angle by the gas station at the far end, then walked towards the hardware store, making a mental note to pick up a case of beer on the way back and to get some change for the Scouts selling apples by the door.

Once inside, he passed the power tools and took a left at the gardening section, where he saw Darlene stacking bags of birdseed on the lower shelf. Eugene's sister never quite appeared at home in the red polo shirt of her uniform. She and Gene were the type of people who had looked too mature at twelve and well-used by forty. One would guess Gene was closer to seventy than fifty-two; Darlene fared only a bit better. When she looked up, he acknowledged her by nodding in her direction, then slowed slightly with the intention of easing around her.

"Hey, Jake, got a sec?" Darlene stood up and brushed off her hands on her thighs, bringing his attention to the creases created by jeans that were too tight.

"Sure, Darlene. What's up?"

Jake had always considered Darlene loud, a bit tough, someone who made sure you could hear her when she called you an asshole. Today, he had to strain to catch her words. "Gene's got cancer, got the word on Tuesday. It's in his colon, but they also found a spot in his liver. It don't look good." She stared at the floor and wedged her hands into the front pockets of her pants, catching the denim waistband with her thumbs. "I was wondering if you could spend a bit of time with him."

The muscles of Jake's neck and shoulders tightened, triggering a slight pulsing sensation that settled above his eyes, the beginning of a tension headache. Already his peripheral vision was blurring. Why was she asking him? It wasn't like he and Eugene were buddies. "I'm sorry, Darlene. I know how close you and Gene are, but I'm not sure I'm the right person for him at the moment."

"Well, I'm not. Been down to his place every day to make sure he gets supper. Don't matter what I say, he just sits on the deck, staring at the river. He may talk to you, though. You know, since you've been through it with Maxine."

That was why. She thought he was some kind of an expert, a Dr. Phil or something. Jake concentrated on the hose reels at the end of the aisle while providing canned responses. "I don't really know that much. Maybe he doesn't want to talk about it yet. Just give him some time."

Jake hadn't told a soul that Maxine was dying. They never really mixed much with the neighbours. Besides, it was something he considered a private matter. But someone knew. Things would happen. One day the lawn would be mowed. On other days, casseroles would turn up on the step, in foil containers so he didn't have to worry about returning dishes. Good casseroles too, plenty of meat with pasta and vegetables. And spices, curry and chili powder that made his house smell lived in when he heated them up. They didn't go to waste; Jake didn't believe in letting good food go to waste. He had no idea who repaired the shingles after the storm that knocked out the power for two days. He had only been aware of the darkness and shaving with cold water. By that time Maxine was in the hospital and Jake would leave every morning and return every night like he had put in a long day at work. Lately, these events were seeping into his consciousness, something like cold water into leaky boots. Someone had known about Maxine, but Jake had never figured out who or how they had found out. Eventually, someone else would learn about Eugene. It was what he was waiting for. He developed an incessant curiosity. It was morbid, really; Jake was aware of that. He would frequently stop what he was doing and tilt his head in the direction of Eugene's place, almost as if expecting something, not sure exactly what. Maybe it could be like the bat signal or perhaps a revelation of some sort, anything that confirmed this fact. Hell, he didn't care what. He just didn't like being the only one who knew.

A lime-green Volkswagen pulled up across the road and Elsa MacDonald got out. Her outfit,. depicting several Tweety and Sylvester chase scenes, was hard to miss. Wearing cartoon characters with pink runners and the long braid that trailed down her back were only a couple of her endearing qualities.

"Well, if it isn't Jake Rendell." She closed the car door and started walking in his direction. "Didn't know you lived out this way."

Jake dropped the garden claw and took several long strides to meet her halfway. It didn't matter what she wore, Elsa was always a welcome sight. "Lived here for eighteen years."

"That don't make you a local around here, Jake. You know that."

"Doesn't make me a stranger either."

"True, the neighbours learn to put up with your flaws after eighteen years." She was smiling and extending her hand to shake his, then pulled him into a hug when he reached for it. "How have you been?"

Jake couldn't recall the last time someone had hugged him. Well, he could. It was Maxine's funeral, but he preferred not to remember that particular occasion. "I've been fine. I am fine. Thanks for asking."

"Well, you don't look like you're starving." She held him at arm's length. "In fact, you may want to add a little salad to your diet. But who am I to talk? It's not like anyone would want to see me in spandex."

One of Elsa's many talents was defusing uncomfortable situations. Jake had watched her do it many times at the hospital. She had a way of taking the edge off. Without her, Jake was sure he wouldn't have made it through the difficult times. "You making house calls now or taking your comedy act on the road?"

"Well, you could say it's a bit of both. I have a new position, home care for oncology patients. Gets me out a few days a week and gives me a little air in between."

Jake lowered his voice. "Then I'm guessing you're here for Eugene. I ran into his sister at the hardware store."

Elsa slid her tongue over her top teeth and nodded. "I'll be seeing him every couple of weeks to start. More later on."

"He's taken to sitting out on the deck all night. I don't sleep that well myself, so I hear him at all hours."

"Everyone takes it differently, Jake." She shifted her weight so her body leaned a little to the left. "I really must get going. It's so good to see you. Now that

I know where you live, why don't I come by early next time and you can make me a coffee?"

Watching her walk away, Tweety and Sylvester crinkling across her back, Jake concluded that Elsa was exactly what he needed. Maybe not the revelation he expected, people around here wouldn't know who she was. Appearance-wise, she looked like some innocent, over-zealous grandmother. It was something else. He was off the hook. No more feeling guilty about it. Elsa and Darlene could manage Eugene. Elsa could call in the real experts if necessary, and Jake, well, Jake was free to go about his business with a clear conscience.

Bob Dylan, at maximum volume, and the sweet smell of marijuana were drifting downriver. Jake was pulling out the long strands of grass between the fencing and the lilac bush when Hector Hickerson strolled over.

"I wonder what's got into Gene," he said.

There was something about Hector that always annoyed Jake. Nothing Jake could put into words. Perhaps it was the way he walked, strutted really, or his know-it-all attitude. Or maybe it was that stupid name. What kind of a parent would give a kid a name like that? He was much younger than Jake, and into gadgets, liked to talk about his BlackBerry and big-screen TV. Hector was one of those people that made Jake glad he and Maxine had never had kids.

Hector jerked his head upwards and sniffed several times. "Can't you smell that?"

"Sure I can smell it. What about it?"

"Gene never tokes at home. He keeps his business and personal life separate. Everyone knows that." Hector paused, as if waiting for Jake to comment, then continued. "Gene doesn't have what most people refer to as a real job. He fixes cars, does a bit of roofing and yard work, all under the table. And he has a thriving weed business. Part-time. He plants the stuff in containers, out on Crown land in the summer. No one knows exactly where. Most likely in places cleared for power lines or burnt by forest fires. I'll tell you, he's savvy. Keeps moving it around. The RCMP would love to catch him. You mean that in all the years you've been here you didn't notice how often the cops are at his place?"

It occurred to Jake that there was another reason he disliked Hector. The man was a gossip. "I noticed. I just figured it was none of my business."

To Jake's relief, Hector hadn't thought the conversation through any further and walked away.

The remainder of the afternoon was restless. Sometimes the sun shone with blinding intensity, other times dark clouds muscled their way to the forefront. Jake found himself in the dining room, staring through the glass doors of the china cabinet, trying to remember how many times they'd actually used Maxine's mother's antique dishes. He was sure he could count them on one hand. When he turned around, he thought he saw Maxine, behind the shafts of sunlight coming through the window. Dust motes drifted in the air around her. She looked as though she had never been sick, then disappeared a few seconds later when the clouds returned. "What do I do with them?" he said, sweeping his hand back and unintentionally knocking the side of the cabinet. Inside, standing plates rattled and teacups vibrated in saucers.

Outside there were gunshots, five or six, then silence. From the window, Jake saw Einstein race towards the pen and into the safety of his doghouse. He took two bottles of beer from the fridge and stepped out the back door, carrying them with their necks between his fingers.

Eugene's house had once been a cottage, but it had been raised over thirty years ago to put in a concrete basement. The yellow siding, coated with grey mildew that resembled a thin layer of bird shit, had to be at least that old. Except for the deck, the rest of the place looked older. So the man did yard work and roofing. Jake never suspected. No doubt Darlene did casseroles. "Here," he said, climbing the stairs. The .22 leaned against the railing, the box of bullets stowed under Gene's chair.

Gene took the beer and nodded towards a plastic chair beside him. Jake sat down, opened his bottle and took a sip. They drank quietly, staring at the meandering water. On the far shore, blue jays, voicing their opinions, flitted between the maples. Crows, high up in the spruce trees, argued back. A fish jumped, its body mooning them for a second, then disappeared.

"Guess I should have taken the kids fishing," Gene said a few minutes later.

Jake inhaled, then released his breath, letting it whistle between his teeth. "You know, I don't claim to be an expert, but maybe you don't want to spend your time thinking of should haves. Maybe you should just make it happen. Sell your crop and buy them a plane ticket. Spend a couple of weeks with them. Take them fishing if that's what you want."

As soon as he said it, he regretted it. What gave him the right to tell Eugene what to do? He'd never told Maxine. God knows he'd wanted to.

It started to rain, beginning slow enough that Jake could identify every drop. The echoing of indents in the river. The burst and roll from the waxed surfaces of leaves. Flicks, followed by whispers of absorption into the ground. Muffled slaps each time one hit the wooden deck. Then it started to pour, drowning the individual drops with the rush of many, running through the gutters to resurrect an odour of dead leaves and mud.

Gene's long hair fell forward in wet curls that dripped down the side of his face. He raked it back with his fingers. "Took some shots at that tree earlier," he said, pointing to a large pine between the deck and the river.

Even through the rain, Jake could see that the bark was ripped in several places where the bullets hit. He decided to take a page from Elsa's book and keep things light. "And I thought you were taking potshots at my dog."

Gene turned and looked at Jake. His mouth was twisted up on one side in a half grin, half smirk. "I just felt like fucking hitting something."

Jake was immediately aware of the weight of his drenched clothes, the rigidity of his neck and shoulders, the way his one hand gripped the bottle too tight and the other was clenched into a fist. He placed the bottle on the deck, stood up and reached for Gene's rifle. "May I?" he said.

Gene nodded, amusement still flickering across his face. He watched Jake load the rifle, surprised that Jake knew how, because it was a skill that Gene figured only a certain type of man acquired. He'd never considered Jake to be that type.

It was a skill that Jake hadn't exercised since he was a teen, hunting with his father, half a dozen years before he met Maxine. He dropped in the cartridges, noting with satisfaction that Gene used the safety, then adjusted his stance and raised the barrel, tucking the stock comfortably into his shoulder. He chose an old spruce with a thick trunk, branchless for the bottom ten feet, focused on a spot about five feet off the ground and pulled the trigger. Then he pulled it again, and again, and again, each time taking in the crack of the shot, the splintering of bark, the satisfaction that comes with tearing through exterior layers to reveal what's underneath, shooting until he finished the round.

Christina, After Leotards and Doc Martens

There are bugs in Christina's cupboard, little brown bugs with crusty exteriors like fleas. But they can't be fleas. Fleas don't live in cupboards. Fleas don't crawl comfortably through Uncle Ben's converted rice, somehow managing to enter the bag, which had been folded over three times and clipped with a blue plastic clothespin. They don't glide happily in flakes of rolled oats, waving tiny appendages at their brothers, sisters, and cousins, who are doing the same. Fleas don't eat people food; they're bloodsuckers and live on dogs and cats. Christina still has doubts; the only thing she knows for sure is that these bugs are not cockroaches or ants. They are the devil she doesn't know.

She ponders all this as she scours the shelves with detergent while inhaling a green-apple scent. Maybe she should be using bleach or some sort of spray, but the environment is one of those things she feels guilty about. Her list is long: quality time, perpetually stained toilets, work, sometimes the lack of work, kids, lumpy mashed potatoes, store-bought cookies and now bugs in the cupboard, just to name a few.

For supper, Christina had planned to make rice because it was faster than potatoes and she was running late. She doesn't make ordinary rice, as everyone finds it pale and uninspiring. Instead she makes yellow rice, coloured and flavoured with a little chicken stock and a lot of curry. Nose-running spicy rice, a family favourite that quickly disappears from pots and plates, a creation she is proud of.

"Pour a cup of rice in the measuring pitcher, please," she'd asked Sara. Christina now regrets those words. She wishes that she had discovered the vagrants herself and quietly disposed of them when no one was looking.

Her daughter is fifteen and has spent the last two years moving from baggy jeans to bum-hugging skirts, while daring to pass judgment on the rest of the world. According to Melissa's mother, she also has a boyfriend, a seventeen-year-old string bean with greasy hair, the type of guy who doesn't look a mother in the eye. Melissa is Sara's best friend. Her mother and Christina have a pact to share information. Christina caught a glimpse of the bean a few weeks ago when she picked up Sara from the mall. Alarm bells have been going off in her head ever since.

Sara shrieked and dropped the measuring cup as bodies began surfacing in the oblong grains. It landed in the kitchen sink, both creatures and rice scattering across stainless steel. Can they swim? Christina wondered, turning on the tap.

Further investigation revealed the rice, flour, and oats were infested, and the cupboard was crawling. "This is so disgusting," Sara said. "Don't you ever clean?" As if it was Christina's fault, and only Christina's fault. Sara stormed out of the kitchen with a look of horror on her face.

What Christina considers disgusting are the oven fries she makes to replace the yellow rice.

"Don't worry, she'll get over it," Robert says. Bugs don't bother him. He is Mr. Boy Scout. Mr. Great Outdoors, the man she used to camp with in tents that spiders loved. They tolerated ants, wasps, horseflies, and mosquitoes in order to catch fish and spy on deer and beaver from their canoe. The kids don't like camping; the boys long for their video games and Sara mopes, loudly. The tent, damp and mouldy after their last miserable trip, was put at the curb with the garbage two years ago.

At Zellers, Christina fills her cart with plastic containers, in all shapes and sizes, to hold everything from flour to instant onion soup. Her neighbour, Paula Spence, literally runs into her en route to the checkout. Paula looks too coordinated, like she just stepped out of a Sears flyer. Maybe she failed to stop because she was too busy admiring her outfit in the glass doors of the pop cooler.

"Oh, hi," she offers, as if an apology isn't necessary when the collision is with someone you know. "Those on sale?"

"No," Christina says, rubbing her sideswiped hip. "I've been cleaning cupboards."

"I absolutely hate cleaning cupboards." Paula admits. "I only do it when they get so disgusting that I can't stand them any longer."

"Me too," Christina says, but she has the sinking feeling that Paula's definition of disgusting doesn't include bugs.

Sara enters the kitchen after school with contempt further clouding her disposition. "What's there to eat in this place that comes in a sealed package?" She says this looking down, her hair falling forward to hide the appearance of bravado mixed with fear. She is pretending it isn't directed towards anyone in particular, although her mother is the only other person in the room.

"Well, if you don't like this restaurant, you can always go eat at Shelby's in the plaza by Blockbuster Video. According to the paper, there was a problem with mice last year, but I'm sure it's okay now." According to Christina's memory, they had had their own mice problem. Almost every morning between April and November, Robert had emptied and reset the trap hidden behind the furnace. Mice, she thought, whose fault is that?

At dinner, Sara picks through her pasta, leaving anything she can't identify on the side of her plate.

Christina watches the pile grow, knowing it contains tarragon and basil, things Sara has eaten before but doesn't know the names of.

"How's business?" Robert asks. He leans forward, intentionally trying to distract her.

"Take a look at my office. It's much too neat to be productive. I have some package shots to close-crop for Medi-Nourish and I'm expecting the Richardson job sometime next week. These slow days make me restless."

"You could learn to enjoy your slow times."

"You could clean," Sara interjects. Her gaze and her fork continue to dissect the food on her plate.

Everyone stops chewing. Jeremy and Graham, both younger than Sara, stare at Christina. A line has been crossed.

"Go to your room," Robert says before Christina can reply.

Sara bangs her dishes on the counter and slams her bedroom door. The rest of the meal is silent except for utensils cautiously wearing against plates, and glasses being set down after muted sips. What would Christina say anyway? Would she launch into one of those when-I-was-your-age lectures, or explode in a defensive rage, camouflaged by a rant about how untidy Sara's bedroom is? She doesn't know.

"Sara hates me," Christina says to Robert while undressing for bed.

"It's just a phase." He slides his hands down her hips. His wedding ring feels cold and goosebumps rise on her skin.

"Lock the door," she says.

Christina spent her sixteenth birthday doing housecleaning during one of her mother's semiannual bucket brigades. Every nook and cranny, closet and shelf had to be scrubbed. How dare her mother steal her milestone, one of the most important days of her young life, for the sake of fall housecleaning? "After all," she had wanted to yell so loud that the echo reverberating from across the lake would emphasize her point, "fall lasts three months."

Several months later, her best friend Suzanne celebrated her sixteenth with a sleepover, a roomful of girls who tittered at thoughts of school dances, makeup, boys, and sex. Christina didn't titter. She lay on an inflatable mattress with cramps that she blamed on overindulgence in homemade chocolate sundaes. The following morning she had her first period. "Better late than never," her mother said, handing her a box of pads that had been stashed in the linen closet for five years.

Sitting at her computer working in Photoshop, Christina guides and clicks the mouse, creating vector points and Bezier curves around the contours of a bottle, some kind of tube-feeding solution the colour of milky tea. Flip open the lid, attach the pump and — voilà — dinner. She has adopted an attitude of crude humour towards these products. It is either that or spend too much time thinking about what it must be like to be old or sick, with nothing but ugly bottles to look forward to. Jean

Pierre, their overweight chocolate Lab, has positioned himself under her desk and is resting his head on his front paws, just inches from her feet. Every few minutes he releases a sound, either a sigh or a snort, to remind her that she has yet to take him for a walk.

In the corner of her office is a drafting table stacked with papers. A T-square and angles lean against the wall next to boxes of dockets and proofs. She stopped using them about the same time that she stopped wearing leotards and Doc Martens. Sometimes that doesn't feel like so long ago. Sometimes it feels like an eternity. Christina had taken to the computer easily. Several friends from art college had rebelled against the new technology that stormed their industry in the late eighties. In the end, many were jobless or had to hire someone else to execute their work. She, at least, maintained a client base — maybe not the most exciting clients, but paying clients nonetheless.

"Enough of this," she mutters after cropping several images. She rolls the chair back and stands up, startling Jean Pierre, who has fallen into doggy dreams. He yelps, as if she'd just run over his paws with the casters. "Come on, we may as well go for that walk."

She stops to check the cupboard on the way to the back door. There are a couple of stray bugs wandering between the new plastic containers for flour and brown sugar. She squishes them with her thumb before washing their crusty bodies down the drain.

When she returns, there is a message on her answering machine: "Christina, Jack Richardson. Call me." Talk about short and sweet. She presses the speed dial.

"Jack, it's Christina."

"I need you to send the illustration files for our instruction books to Simon Kent at Kent Graves."

"An agency. I thought you were happy with my work."

"Don't take it personal, Christina. Simon is the Chair of the Board of Trade Marketing Committee. We have the same tee-off time at the club."

"Are you telling me I should take up golf?" Christina has never felt so diminished in her life.

Dinner is safe: pork chops, mashed potatoes, and frozen peas.

"Good potatoes," says Graham.

"Yeah, Mom, good potatoes," Jeremy says, mimicking his brother, except that he just stuffed a forkful into his mouth and they are beginning to coagulate.

"Jeremy, you're so gross. Didn't anyone ever tell you that you're not supposed to talk with your mouth full?" Sara's voice has that self-appointed-expert tone, as if she now considers herself the authority on all things revolting. "Dad, there's some papers in the living room that I need you to sign."

"Don't you think I should read them first?"

"Sure, if you want. Melissa asked me to sleep over. Can I?"

"What do you think, Christina? Can she?"

Christina knows that he wants to roll his eyes, but Sara is watching. Instead, he shoves a forkful of peas into his mouth, then bends over to retrieve two that fall on the floor.

When Robert leaves to drive Sara to Melissa's, Christina asks him to detour to the liquor store for a six-pack and a large bottle of red wine. "Make it a screw top," she says. The two boys park themselves in front of the PlayStation in the family room. Grunts and the sounds of imaginary weapons drift up the stairs and attest to their activities. On the coffee table Christina sees Sara's papers, two tests (requiring signatures), and a form for Take Your Kid to Work Day, already completed with Robert's job information.

"Ahhhh, wine," she says, reaching for the bottle as soon as Robert returns. "I'll pour?"

The walls of her doctor's office are the colour of sweat-stained undershirts. They make Christina want to puke. She is there for the results of her tests. Last week she told Mildred that she wasn't feeling quite right. That something was wrong, but she couldn't put her finger on it.

"Well," says Mildred, "we've ruled out premenopause."

"Considering I was a late bloomer, that's nice to know."

"Your tests indicate that you're pregnant."

"Oh," says Christina, cupping her hand over her mouth as the room begins to spin, "I think I'm going to be sick."

"I can't believe that you could make this kind of stupid mistake," Sara shrieks when Christina and Robert announce the news. "This is so disgusting. You two are old." She lectures them as if she is the parent, tossing in words like responsible, adult and birth control. This time Christina wants to roll her eyes but pours herself a glass of milk instead. From behind the frosted glass rim, she watches Robert hold a straight face. Later, they will lock the bedroom door, crawl under the duvet, and giggle like chastised teens.

In her fifth month, Christina pours chocolate sauce over a dish of brownie delight ice cream, then sprinkles it with pecans and drops on a maraschino cherry. She's in the mood to celebrate. Yesterday, she acquired a new client, sent to her by Jack Richardson. Guilt, she figures. The infestation of her kitchen is over, and her second trimester is progressing nicely. Everyone is excited at the prospect of a new brother. Everyone except Sara, that is. She has yet to come around. These days, Christina worries a bit less about her daughter. It has something to do with the subtle differences in her appearance — skirts not as tight, makeup not as thick. Melissa's mother just called to say that the string bean was history, definitely reason to celebrate. Still, there is the guilt over the fact that her unexpected pregnancy bothers Sara so much. She scoops a large spoonful of ice cream, making sure to include the cherry and copious amounts of sauce and pecans, then proceeds to seduce her taste buds by moving the spoon in and out of her mouth, savouring the flavour bit by bit. By the time she has finished her dessert, she realizes that all the chocolate sauce in the world won't alleviate this guilt; and she stares out the window wondering if she will ever have a relationship with her daughter again.

A Breath Before the Collision

Occasionally, between the end of the grey drizzle and the start of blackfly season, there is one of those rare April days that brings everyone, long weary of being inside, out of their homes. Some people emerge in shorts because the weather gives the illusion of late May or even June, and they want to rush the season forward. Front doors are left open and windows are raised, enabling the outside to also journey in. It is as though each house has taken the sleeves of its winter coat and pulled them back through the armholes to expose the lining. Such a day doesn't happen every year, only when there is a slight pause between the grey and the black, like a breath before the collision.

Megan, looking older than her forty-seven years, is not the first person out this Saturday morning, although she is early. Strands of hair, both brown and grey, flip and curl out from under the ball cap she wears. She is tall and gaunt, almost witch-like in appearance. That's how many of the local children see her. Below her eyes sit shadows of blue-black, like someone who is ill or deprived of sleep. The knee is torn in her denim overalls; her shirt is faded and stained.

The people across the road are also out and stop raking their lawn in order to chat with the people who live in the house to their left. Megan doesn't bother getting to know the neighbours any more. There was a time when she knew them all, but that was years ago. Everyone from those days has moved on. The neighbourhood has always been considered affordable, good starter homes for couples with young families, or first-time investments for up-and-comers.

She and John had been so happy to find the L-shaped bungalow with water frontage that fell within their price range. During the two-month closing period, they drove by on several occasions, hardly able to contain their excitement. Then came moving day, their apartment belongings packed up and placed into the various rooms of their new home, which still looked empty after their meagre furnishings arrived. "Room to expand," John had said, and she agreed.

Megan especially remembers the first person she and John had met when they arrived on the picturesque crescent. It was Evelyn Montgomery, appearing instantly upon the departure of the moving van, a bucket and sponge in one hand and a plate of sandwiches in the other, as if she had been watching from the side window of her own house and waiting for that very moment, which she admitted some time later that she had been. It was her way to get involved and help out. A couple of years later, it was Evelyn who showed Megan how to express the milk from her engorged breasts so Jamie could latch on when they came home from the hospital. She was a nurse, her husband Rob a contractor. Builders and fixers, Megan called them.

Together, Evelyn and Megan had organized charity drives and community events and garden tours and a book club, which started a small controversy because their first novel, *The Wars*, hit a nerve with Celeste Rogers, who stated that she could not read past *that part*, the one with Taffler and the Swede. "That's not the issue," Evelyn had said. "The story is about finding ways to cope with a horrific event while feeling totally isolated. That part just helps to make the point." But Celeste couldn't agree.

Megan tried to turn the conversation around by saying, "Look at it from a different perspective. It's about being at the mercy of strangers. Robert is always at the mercy of people he doesn't feel close to. His own mother is the biggest stranger in his life, the worst offender. It was she who drove him to enlist. You're aware of that from early on." Then she chuckled. "It's always the mother's fault. Did you ever notice that?"

"Yes," replied Evelyn, laughing, "the mother or the butler, depending on circumstances." After that, *it must have been the butler* was their standing private joke, sending them spiralling into uncontrollable laughter while John and Rob looked on perplexed.

That was forever ago. Nowadays, Megan prefers to converse with Findley, a Heinz-57 mutt with one brown eye and one blue, who speaks very little in return, just the way Megan likes it. He follows her to the garage, where she picks up an expanding bucket and her gardening gloves. The garage has never held a car but assumes the role of shed and attic combined. In the corner closest to the door are tools and pots with dead houseplants. Off to one side sits a baby's crib, its corners and bars draped with spider webs. The accompanying mattress, once bright with printed lambs and rabbits, is now stained with mildew. Some boxes contain university textbooks, old and outdated. Others hold household items, some old, some just no longer used. Findley sniffs the floor where some mouse droppings lie, then follows the scent, only to lose it under a pile of discards that lean against one wall.

"Come on, Fin, let's go," Megan says. Then she and the dog stroll around the side of the house towards the backyard.

To the people on the street, Megan is an oddity. Eccentric, some call her. Others say she is a free spirit. What they do agree on is that her yard is a mess. For the amount of time that she spends outside, it never appears to them that anything improves. The front lawn, mostly dandelions and wild strawberries, always has notable dead spots that they believe must be cinch bugs but are actually where Findley does his business, burning the weeds with his urine. The gardens are overgrown, with no divisions between plants that they can see. Thyme invades the phlox. Snow-in-summer intrudes on the coreopsis. Black-eyed Susans, allowed to go to seed, sprout up in the middle of everything. On this April day, the chaos is less apparent because these things have yet to wake up. The neighbours, too busy with their own yards and social niceties, have not yet cast a disapproving eye in Megan's direction. This will happen later, in summer, provoking whispers and nods and discussions on patios or at community events. "Thank heavens the house is brick and the windows are vinyl. Imagine what the place would look like if they weren't."

The backyard slopes gracefully to the lake. It is more like a large pond, rather shallow and weedy, not really big enough for boats or summer recreation, a perfect habitat for birds and bugs. Gardens stretch in both directions towards the property line from a walk that winds its way down to the water. The faces of early pansies stare upwards from between the stones in a defiant manner. *Pick us out, we dare you.* Others would have, but Megan likes the violet flowers and lets them be. She is not one who thinks of them as weeds or who cares that they have decided to live in the cracks of her garden path.

She begins at the top of the hill, cleaning out the dead leaves from last fall, a job she prefers to do in the spring to avoid the chill of autumn once they fall from the trees. Findley sits on the walk, watching her while she gathers them, some dry and crackling, others wet and full of the movement of wood bugs. Each time she fills the bucket, Megan walks back up the slope and dumps it in a pile at the side of the yard where they will remain, eventually becoming overgrown with tall grass and bugleweed.

"Fin, where's your ball?" she says, and the dog begins searching the yard for the toy, wavering back and forth with his nose to the ground and his tail in the air.

Megan pulls out the stems of last year's day lilies. They are hollow and always make her think of Huck Finn hiding in the river and using a reed to breathe while under water. At least she thinks it was Huck Finn. Perhaps it was from an old movie she saw once, perhaps both. She puts all the stems into the bucket, then moves on to the hostas to do the same, slowly working her way from side to side, stopping to check individual perennials for new growth. One of her coral bells has died. Its brittle stock and root lifts out of the ground with a handful of leaves that Megan scoops up. A beetle scurries over the clumps of loose dirt and an earthworm pulls its body back into a dark tunnel.

Jamie died when he was three. If Megan allowed it, she could still see his lifeless body and his crushed tricycle under the rear wheel of the pickup. The black Ford pickup with a black cap that made her remember it like a hearse. Blue trike. Yellow hair. Red blood. Both she and John were standing at the fence talking to Evelyn. Jamie was riding his trike up and down the driveway. "Look, Mommy, look, Daddy, look at me," he called over and over and they would look and clap and tell him how great he was doing. It was one of those rare April days. Rob jumped into his truck and shouted that he was going to get fertilizer for the lawn. Somewhere in a single breath of time, unseen by four sets of eyes, Jamie turned his tricycle onto the sidewalk and raced towards the Montgomerys' driveway. "Look, Mommy, look, Daddy, look at me."

Jamie!

Megan inhales deeply through her nose and exhales through the circle of her mouth, as if in labour. Findley nudges her with his muzzle, holding the ball between his teeth. "Hey, Fin, you found it," she says, rubbing the dog's ears. For a moment, she holds him around the neck and rests her cheek against his soft head, then stands up and grabs the bucket by the handle. "Let's go to the lake."

Mayflies are hatching from the water. Their vertical wings carry them upwards and away from their nymph relatives. Such unusual creatures, with upright appendages and dual wire tails. They look like something from a cover of the fantasy novels John used to read, something that would have a warrior sitting on its back holding reins with one hand and waving a sword with the other. Jamie would have loved the mayflies. By the age of three, he had been immersed in a world of knights and castles. He would be sixteen now, spending too much time on the computer or playing video games and talking on the phone with his friends. Probably a reader like both parents, and possibly involved in sports or music.

At first, there had been the drug-induced numbness that carried them through the funeral and the weeks after, the sedatives making their mouths so dry that every swallow felt like they were forcing the entire world down. It would only go so far, then stick like a goitre in their throats. Afterwards, the distribution of blame, no names spoken, no eye contact made, only what-if scenarios that crowded their thoughts. When the Sold sign went up on Evelyn and Rob's front lawn, they were both relieved. There was the night that Megan sat with her back leaning against the locked bathroom door. The remaining sedatives dumped from the amber vial between her spread legs while she counted them. Seventeen. John pounding on the other side, the vibrations of his force rocking her shoulder blades, "Megan, are you okay?" then apologizing when the toilet flushed as she watched the pills circle the bowl. Grabbing the towels, she opened the door and walked past him to take them to the laundry room.

Megan takes the orange ball from the dog's mouth and pitches it into the lake. It bobs to the surface, surrounded by successive rings. Findley jumps in and begins to swim while she picks up more debris. When he returns to shore, his wet fur is weighted into points that hang dripping from his body. He shakes them out before bringing the ball to her. She tosses it again and he swims off to retrieve it. The next time she throws it, it lands further out in the water. Findley looks at it, turns back towards her and lets out a slow whine, his odd eyes searching her for direction.

"Don't give me that look. Go get it." The dog whines again. "Oh, stop it and go get your ball," she says, turning her back and breaking off the dead stalks of astilbes. Findley paces back and forth, little whimpers escaping from his throat. He raises his front paw and touches Megan on the thigh. "Findley, you're such a suck." She picks up a rock and throws it out to where the ball floats in the lake. Findley goes after the rock and returns with the orange sphere in his mouth.

That's what John hated, her tough exterior, that and her silence. When he screamed and threw things, she walked away. When he cried in his sleep, she moved to the sofa. She saw him the other day at the mall. He had two children with him. A girl of six who must get all her looks from her mother, and a younger boy with Jamie's complexion and hair but someone else's smile. They made small talk while blinking away the echoes of their former lives, then parted with promises to get together they both knew would never be kept.

Findley occupies himself with the ball at the shoreline, batting it with his paw and pushing it through the mud with his nose. Megan kneels and lifts more brown leaves, holding them in two hands like a mouth of a crane before dropping them into the bucket. Under the pile, several green shoots reach out of the ground. She pauses for a moment to swat the air above her head where she can hear the first blackfly of yet another season.

Fragile Blue and Creamy White

Soft green numbers stared at him from the night table. 4:27, they said. The glow from a streetlight seeped through the slats of the blinds, leaving horizontal bands of darkness between. His eyes scanned the room, adjusting to the half-dark, half-light. Looking around, he saw familiar knickknacks nestled with objects he didn't recognize, furniture that he knew next to pieces that were foreign to him. A strand of silver light settled on the hair of the woman asleep on the next pillow, her breathing creating a nasal rhythm that punctuated the silence. Everything was out of sorts, like a hazy dream, or a foggy reality.

Thirsty, he lifted the bedclothes with caution and swung his legs to the floor. His left hip ached, a constant reminder of the beach at Dieppe, and he leaned on the night table for support. A pair of slippers partially under the bed were visible in the dim light. He nudged them out with his foot and slipped them on, then shuffled out the bedroom door and up the hall.

The kitchen glowed with assorted lights, gadgets, and more numbers, this time 4:42. He ran his hand through his hair, which was damp with his perspiration, and looked around, surveying the room with its boxy white appliances and yellow paint. Lace curtains hung on the window above the sink and herb pots sat on the ledge. It all seemed wrong, not the kitchen he remembered.

He began searching for a glass behind cupboard doors, finding one on the third try, and opened the refrigerator, hoping that it held a jug of ice-cold water like the one in the kitchen he was more familiar with. Thankfully it did. Filling the glass, he gulped it down and poured another, taking it with him to the table that stood next to the bay window overlooking the yard. He sat, leaned on his elbows and rested his forehead in the palms of his hands, closed his eyes and stayed still for a long time.

The morning light reached across the back garden and into the window, settling on the table and floor. He lifted his head and sipped on the remaining water while scanning the kitchen for something that would help him to orient himself. The confusion and panic stayed, no matter how much he willed them to be gone. His eyes rested on the figure of a jolly chef that hung next to the telephone. Grocery staples: milk, bread, butter, flour, sugar, and eggs were listed down the front of his apron. Little wooden pegs stood in holes at the bottom and could be placed adjacent to each item to mark those to be purchased on the next trip to the store. It was a novelty really, not something anyone used. It had once hung in his mother's kitchen. He and his brother used to drag a chair across the room to stand on so they could move the pegs into different positions when she wasn't looking. She always put them back across the bottom when she cleaned up after dinner. Seeing it, he couldn't help but smile.

Stepping outside, barely lifting his feet, he made his way down the driveway and up Raymoor Avenue while surveying the neighbourhood, noting any changes in house colours, or additions like sheds and gazebos. He had lived on this street since he was a boy and had never tired of it.

The big house had always been grey with white gingerbread and railings. As he followed the walkway leading to the front veranda, he noted that the petunias in the garden needed deadheading and the hardy geraniums could use a thinning out. He rang the bell, then waited a minute and rang again. Inside, the chime of a clock marked the half hour. A silhouette moved behind frosted sidelights and the deadbolt shifted to the unlocked position. Finally, he thought, releasing his breath just before looking into the face of the stranger standing beyond the security chain on the partiallyopened door. "Who are you?" he cried, his panic increasing tenfold. "Where's my mother? Where's Robina Winslow?"

"Phillip, is that you? What are you doing out this early in the morning?" The man was middle-aged, with thinning hair, but fit. He stood in bare feet, adjusting a navy robe tied loosely at his waist.

Turning, Phillip trudged back along the cement path that led to the street, avoiding the cracks between the grey slabs like children do when they play. *Step on a crack, break your mother's back.* He sat down on the curb, his bent knees rising upwards from the pavement like crests of hills, and tears flowed down his cheeks.

The sound of the ringing phone startled her, waking her with the feeling that only seconds had passed since she had closed her eyes. Picking up the receiver, she glanced in his direction. His pillow was empty, the bedclothes pulled back.

"Hello?"

"Emma, it's Geoff Chambers."

"Yes, Geoff, what can I do for you?" She fingered the night table in search of her glasses, knocking a pencil to the floor before locating them on the other side of her crossword book, then fumbled with one hand to open them and set them in place so she could see the time. Just after six thirty.

"It's Phillip. He's sitting on the curb in front of our house. He came to the door looking for his mother."

"Oh, dear, I'll be right there."

"I'll keep an eye on him until you get here."

"Thank you, and thank you for calling."

She pulled on the pair of elastic-waist pants that she kept near the bed, slipping them up under her cotton nightdress before lifting it over her head. With equal efficiency, she put on her bra and hooked it from behind, then pulled on a shirt and donned a pair of ankle socks and walking shoes.

The street was empty and still cool from the night. She hurried past the post-war houses at the north end towards the older Victorians that stood stately on the south. These days she was slower and slightly stooped in her gait, unlike in her youth when she had perfect posture and a bounce in her step. Now she often felt old and tired, slow and stooped. Or was it stupid? Yes, there were days that she just felt stupid. On other days she was angry, either with Phillip or herself.

She saw him in front of the old house, sitting like a lost little boy with his head resting on his arms, which were folded across the tops of his knees. That's what he was some days, a little boy, sneaking off and hiding from her, or hiding things from her, afraid she was going to steal them. Just yesterday, he put the keys to the shed in the sugar bowl. It took her hours to find them, and when she did, it was too late to have their grandson mow the lawn.

"Phillip," she said, approaching him gently and placing her hand on his shoulder. "It's time to come home." He looked so helpless, staring at his slippers, at the wet spots where his tears had washed away the dust. She waved to Geoff, who nodded and closed his door.

"It's me, Phillip, Emma, your wife." She placed one hand under his elbow and the other firmly around his upper arm. "Come on, up you go." He was heavy and she could do nothing more than guide him.

"My wife?"

"Yes, Phillip, we've been married over fifty years. Now come on, let's go home and have a nice breakfast. I'll make your favourite, blueberry pancakes."

"Fifty years," he murmured, hesitating slightly before beginning to raise himself from the curb.

Keeping a firm grip on his arm, Emma chose not to respond. She was thinking of that grey January day when she had stood in a borrowed white dress and he'd had a sprig of heather pinned on his uniform; and of her arrival aboard *The Queen Mary*, pregnant with the twins, only they didn't know there were two babies at the time; and of his mother's comments on her advanced size when she stepped off the train and they met her at Union Station. Then there was the drive all the way from downtown Toronto to Markham, which was nothing more than a village; and the dust that flew into her eyes and mouth through the open windows of the old car; and the doubts that overwhelmed her the closer they came, and that didn't leave until that night when Phillip crawled under the covers of the bed in the small room they shared across the hall from his parents.

"Sit here and read while I make breakfast," she said, installing him in his worn recliner and handing him a copy of *The Economist* that was over a week old.

He was submissive and took the paper from her hands. She knew his disorientation rendered him helpless, and that he wouldn't read, just hide behind the newspaper and pretend to be reading. She could tell that he didn't like the way she looked at him, that he was thinking he would never have married such a woman, one who was serious and stern and told him what to do. It was as if she could read his thoughts through his hollow eyes.

In the kitchen, the blueberries were washed and draining in the colander. The sun lit the yellow walls in what she had once described as a cheerful manner. "Imagine, another election so soon," she said, talking as she scooped flour into a measuring cup and levelled the top with a butter knife. "I really don't think those politicians care one way or another what we think." She added a second cup of flour to the stainless steel bowl along with a couple of teaspoons of baking powder, some sugar and salt. "It's supposed to be hot again today. Another one for the tomatoes." She laughed, adding a little singsong quality to her words. "You know how they love the heat. I'll be putting up both chili and chow this year. I realized that yesterday when I checked on them. We're going to have tomatoes coming out our ears.

"The vegetable garden needs weeding. We could do it this morning before it gets too hot, if you like." She continued chattering, bringing up additional tidbits gleaned from the news, or making references to the children and their families, all the while stirring the batter with a wooden spoon that was as old as her marriage. She glanced at the clock on the microwave. Only 7:20 and already she had checked it four times.

Gently she folded the berries into the batter, careful not to over-mix and break the fragile blue into the creamy white. Then she scooped four heaping spoonfuls into the electric frying pan. The recipe would make about a dozen pancakes, some for breakfast, some for the freezer. She put the coffee on, keeping her eye on the circles in the pan, waiting for the air bubbles pop.

"Breakfast is ready," she called, setting the plates on the table. "I've given you three pancakes to start, but there are more if you want." Two glasses of orange juice followed, carefully set to the right of each plate.

The comforting smells from the kitchen enticed Phillip and made him eager. Slamming the recliner into the upright position, he bounded to the table and began hoeing into breakfast as if he hadn't eaten in a week.

Forks and knives against china plates, sips from juice and the occasional clicking of false teeth, the sounds of a silent breakfast between strangers.

After they finished eating, Emma cleared the plates and poured the coffee. "So, do you feel like weeding the garden today?"

"No, I feel like visiting my mother."

"Oh, Phillip." She sighed, laying her hand over his. "Your mother has been gone for twenty-three years."

"How would you know?" he yelled, shock and anger and hatred crossing his face. He jumped up from the table, knocking over a mug of coffee in the process. The scalding liquid poured over her wrist. "How dare you!" he said, storming down the hall and flinging open the front door, which banged against the stop as he left the house for the second time that morning in his pyjamas.

Emma turned on the kitchen tap to run cold water on her wrist, deciding she would give him a minute to calm down before going after him. Perhaps she could convince him to take a nap on the daybed in the spare room. If she put on some old music, he might sleep for two or three hours. Perhaps she should call the doctor and begin the arrangements. It takes time for these things, for checkups and waiting lists, for everyone to get used to the idea.

He was shuffling along the sidewalk, going away from his mother's old house instead of towards it. She watched and followed him, keeping a distance of several driveways. They passed lawns that were tired and burnt from the August drought, the same lawns their children had played on when everyone on the street knew each other.

When he turned into the park, she stopped at the entrance, absently rubbing her scalded wrist as she watched him walk past a bench, then turn back and sit down facing the swings. It was early and the playground was quiet. Shadows in shapes of extended triangles reached out towards his slippers. She observed him for a few minutes longer before approaching.

"Hello, Phillip," she said, keeping her voice even.

"There you are." He was smiling now and looking up at her. "You know, I've always liked it here. This place never changes."

"Yes," she said. It's nice here." She sat next to him on the bench, careful not to say or do anything that could disrupt his calm state.

"I brought the twins here once," he said, "when they were little. Peter wanted to be spun on the swings so I turned him around and around until the chains were tight, then let him go. He got dizzy and threw up. Afterwards he started to cry. I never told you that. Figured you'd say I was being irresponsible. I probably was. We sat here and I held him on my lap for a long time while Anne played. I think he liked that, being held."

Emma tucked her arm through Phillip's and rested her head on his shoulder. He placed his hand on her thigh, stroking it in a reassuring manner. Morning traffic moved through the streets. Insects rose lazily from the grass. Two crows flew overhead. Somewhere a dog barked. "Would you like some breakfast?" she said. "I've made your favourite, blueberry pancakes."

Acknowledgements

Earlier versions of many of these stories have appeared in the following publications, to which I am extremely grateful: "Double Exposure," *Riddle Fence*, Fall 2013; "Billy," *The Antigonish Review*, Fall 2012; "Christina, After Leotards and Doc Martens," *Qwerty*, Spring 2011; "Thomas and the Woman,"*Grain*, Winter 2011, awarded First Place in *Grain*'s 22nd Annual Short Story Contest; "Chasing Rabbits," *Wascana Review*, online 2010; "Beverly Innes," *The Antigonish Review*, Winter 2010; "Stepsister," *All Rights Reserved*, Fall 2009; "Prerequisites for Sleep," *carte blanche*, online, Fall 2009; *Canadian Content*, seventh edition, 2011; "Knowing," *The Fiddlehead*, Summer 2009; "Fragile Blue and Creamy White," *FreeFall*, Summer 2009; "A Breath Before the Collision," *Other Voices*, Fall 2008.

I also wish to express my appreciation to all the editors/publishers, whether they published my work or not, who took the time to provide feedback to help make me a better writer.

About the Author

Jennifer L. Stone left Nova Scotia for Toronto in 1981. It wasn't until she returned, seventeen years later, and saw her home province as an outsider, that she was inspired to begin writing. Her fiction has appeared in numerous literary journals including: *The Fiddlehead, The Antigonish Review, Grain, Other Voices, FreeFall, carte blanche, All Rights Reserved, The Wascana Review, Qwerty* and *Riddle Fence*. Her short story "Prerequisites for Sleep" was selected by Nelson Education Ltd. to appear in *Canadian Content*, 7th Edition. In 2010, she was awarded first prize in *Grain*'s 22nd Annual Short Story Contest. A graduate of Ryerson, York University and The Humber School of Writers, she has worked as a designer of advertising inflatables, a software instructor, and currently earns a living as a graphic designer.